King Shifter Queen Fae

WICKED FAE
BOOK FOUR

AMELIA SHAW

KING SHIFTER QUEEN FAE

First edition. July 22, 2023.

Copyright © 2024 Harley Romance Publishing.

Contact: harleyromancepublishing@gmail.com

Website: www.harleyromancepublishing.com

Written by Amelia Shaw

All rights reserved.

No part of this book may be reproduced in any form or by any electronic or mechanical means, including information storage and retrieval systems, without written permission from the author, except for the use of brief quotations in a book review.

This is a work of fiction. Similarities to real people, places, or events are entirely coincidental.

Chapter 1
AURELIA

THE CRUSHING weight of losing Zeke bore down on me as Grey skidded to a stop outside.

"Damn it." Grey dropped me to the ground, and I landed on my feet and spun to see the problem.

Secret Service agents surrounded us with their hands on their weapons. They weren't going to let us get away. I stared one of them down, but there was something off about the man's eyes. They were oddly blank.

I glanced back at the doors we'd just come through, and my shoulders slumped at what we were leaving behind. Zeke. He'd pissed me off more often than not, but he was my friend and I hated leaving him behind.

Asher clamped a hand on my shoulder. "He would want us to get out of here, Aurelia."

"I know." My voice wobbled.

"Then stop looking back when the fight is in front of us. You've gotta survive this." He nudged me forward.

"How are we going to get out of here?" I asked, glancing around.

Grey ran a hand down his face. "I don't know how we can without using magic against the humans."

"That's our only option," Dan said.

One of the agents stepped forward, his eyes glassy like all the others. "Come with us quietly and no one else needs to get hurt."

"Yeah, right," I growled. "Your bosses plan to murder us the same way you did Zeke."

I pooled magic in my palms. It wasn't the solution I wanted at all. I hated the idea of using magic against humans, but we needed to get out of here.

I peered over at Grey, and he nodded his head in confirmation.

"I don't want to use my magic on them any more than you do, but it's the only way." He clenched his hands into fists.

Weapons were drawn, and the men surrounding us aimed their guns but didn't move to shoot us.

"Using magic against us is illegal. You will be tried and put to death," the agent in front said.

He took another step closer. Grey growled low in his throat. His eyes glowed with his wolf. Grey, Ash and Dan formed a tight circle around me, even though I was the most powerful among them.

"Overprotective men," I whispered under my breath.

Grey shot me a wink. His oversensitive wolf ears picked up everything, including my annoyance at the men protecting me. I took a step forward, but Grey blocked me.

"What are you doing?" he asked.

"Fighting. We need to get out of here before more of them show up." I rolled my eyes and nudged him to the side.

"Stop."

That voice was one I knew all too well. How did he evade us inside the event? I spun on my heel to face Malcolm, who stood at the top of the steps at the exit of the building from which we'd fled.

"I need them alive!" he barked.

The Secret Service agents holstered their weapons and lunged for us as one. My shadows writhed up my arms to my hands and shot out at the leader as he rushed me, trapping him in chains.

"How did we miss him in there?" I asked. "I didn't see him anywhere."

"It doesn't matter," Asher grunted. "We need to get out of here."

He tossed the man he was grappling with over his shoulder, and the man gasped as he landed on his back. Two more men rushed Ash with a battle cry, and he roundhouse kicked them both, one after the other.

"Aurelia, behind you!" Grey screamed.

I ducked and spun around in a sweeping kick, taking my attacker off his feet, and jumped up into a fighting stance.

The Secret Service agents outnumbered us four to one. The odds of us getting out of here without using magic on the humans were terrible. I let my natural magic fill my palms and prayed that what I wanted to do would work before flinging the magic at the men closest to me.

That magic hit the first one in the chest, and his eyes rolled back in his head as he fell into the man next to him. He was out like a light, but I just hoped I'd only knocked him out and didn't kill him.

There was no time to worry about that though, as three more men rushed forward to take his place. Ash stepped up behind me and plastered his back to mine.

"You need someone at your back, Princess. They seem to be gunning for you specifically," Ash said.

"Yeah, I think that's Malcolm's influence," I mumbled and threw another ball of magic at the men circling me.

One agent dove out of the way just in time for the ball to miss him, but it hit the man fighting Grey in the back and he toppled over.

Please don't be dead.

Magic was about motive, and I had no intention of killing them, so I had to believe they were just unconscious.

Malcolm bellowed, "Get her! I don't care what you do with the others. I want her."

"He's still an obsessed psycho." I shook my head.

I blasted more of the agents with magic, but the first ones I struck were already starting to wake up. The men took Malcolm's declaration to mean that he didn't care if the others died, and several of them drew their weapons, pointing them at Grey and the others.

Ten agents surrounded Ash and me. Magic built faster in my palms, and I threw it as quickly as it was produced. I knocked out enough of them that I could at least escape the circle in which they'd surrounded me.

"Ash, go help Grey!" I yelled as three agents attacked Grey from all sides.

"No! He'll be pissed if I leave you unprotected," Ash grunted.

I turned at the sound to see a man holding a long, sharp blade that was dripping with Ash's blood. I screamed and launched myself at the man, my hands glowing with a mixture of magic and shadows. I refused to lose anyone else that night.

"You stupid man!" I roared. "You took a knife for me, didn't you?"

I glanced at Ash. There was a rip in both his shirt and jacket. A small line of blood dripped from the thin laceration.

"Aurelia, watch out!" Ash bellowed.

The distraction cost me.

The man slashed at me, and pain seared through my chest, burning agony lighting all my limbs on fire. The man grinned at me. He wasn't like the other agents. His eyes were cold and cruel. He yanked the blade from my stomach just as my magic hit him in the chest.

He screamed as he flew back, and the shadows ate away at his skin. It was gruesome. The shadows burned away the fabric and melted his skin until bones and tendons could be seen under the charred flesh.

I nearly puked but got to my feet and spun away from the true horror that my magic could inflict on another person. I'd done that. My magic was something truly terrifying, but I didn't have time to break down over what I'd just done.

I had wanted the man to hurt just as badly as he'd hurt me. Did that make me a terrible person? I shook off the thoughts. I could unpack that later.

Blood dripped down the front of my dress, but my wound would heal soon enough. I turned to find more agents with long blades. They clearly weren't human but rather Fae pretending to be Secret Service. One of them slashed at Grey, and he jumped back.

Pain echoed in the wound left by the Fae guard. It pulsed, and blood continued its steady stream from the wound. It should have started healing already. Maybe it was just the adrenaline of the fight keeping the blood pumping out of me.

I couldn't stop though. I had to keep fighting, no matter what. We had to get out of here. Everything depended on us escaping this mess, but we were still outnumbered, and more agents continued to flood the streets.

I'd lost sight of Grey and Dan in the commotion as I spun, kicking out at a guard. Blood gushed from his side as my stiletto pierced his skin. I shoved him away from me and searched for Grey and Dan.

There were too many enemies and not enough allies. How the hell were we going to get out of this?

Something hit me like a battering ram and shoved me to the side. I blinked up at Ash from where I'd landed on my ass. He punched an agent in the face, and a crack filled the air as the man's nose gushed blood and he fell to the ground, limp.

Ash reached a hand out to me. His knuckles were cracked and bleeding. He pulled me to my feet, and I nodded gratefully.

A sharp pain sliced through my back, and it arched as I screamed. More blood gushed from my back as I stumbled forward into Ash. He shoved me behind him and disarmed the agent in a swift move before slicing the blade across the man's throat with a bellow of rage.

Tears pricked at my eyes, and I pressed a hand to the gash on my back. It came away wet with blood. I stumbled sideways. I wasn't healing as fast as I should have been.

Why am I not healing?

Arms banded around me from behind, locking my arms to my sides. Whoever had me lifted me from my feet, and I kicked back with the pointy heel of my shoe, catching him in the shin.

"Stop fighting!" the man bellowed.

I kicked him again and again as I thrashed in his hold. My shadows swirled along my arms and slid like tar on to the man where his arms were tight around me. He screamed as the shadows burned away the cloth on his suit jacket and melted his skin beneath.

"Aurelia!" Grey roared as the man dropped me to the ground.

The agent batted at the shadows as he continued to scream. I hated it. I hated having to use my magic that way. I stumbled back to my feet. Grey was fighting to get to me but there were too many guards rushing toward me now.

Dan appeared at my side with a blade in each hand. He must have stolen them from the agents he fought. He handed one to me.

"Thank you. I hate using my magic like that." I took the blade and held it out.

I slashed at anything that came close to me, but the only agents who would even come near the blade were the ones with blank eyes. The others carefully kept their distance.

My head spun suddenly, and I jolted to the side, directly into Dan. What was happening to me? I blinked but the ground was uneven, and the night sky swirled around me.

"Aurelia, are you okay?" Dan gripped my shoulders, steadying me.

"I'm dizzy." My words were slurred.

"Shit, you're not healing." Dan glanced down at the hole in my stomach, blood still flowing from it.

"Why am I not healing?" I shook my head.

"You were stabbed. The blade might have something on it to stop the healing process."

"Twice," I said and stumbled again.

"What?" Dan asked and searched my face.

"I was stabbed twice." I dropped to my knees.

I was so tired. My legs couldn't hold me anymore. I fell to the side, and my head smacked into the concrete, pain exploding behind my eyes.

"Grey!" Dan roared. "The princess is injured."

Darkness swirled in my vision. I slapped at the ground, desperate to get up. I needed to help them, but my limbs were so heavy. I was tired. My eyes blinked closed, and darkness engulfed me.

GREY

"GREY, THE PRINCESS IS INJURED!" Dan's words hit me like a sledgehammer.

I spun to him with a bellow. My wolf exploded out of me without my consent, ripping through the agents gleefully and without mercy as he raced to his mate.

Aurelia was pale and her eyes were closed. My wolf nudged her with his nose. She was cool to the touch. I stood over her, snarling in my black wolf form. No one would get to my mate again. I wouldn't allow it.

My wolf barked, and Ash materialized next to me. He growled a warning at the Rider.

"Easy. We need to get out of here. Let me carry her." Asher raised his hands in surrender.

He's a friend. Let him help, I commanded my wolf.

It went against everything my wolf stood for to let someone else touch his mate, but Ash had proven himself time and time again. My wolf nodded his furry head and snarled again at the encroaching agents.

He crouched down, ready to pounce on anyone that got too close to us. Guns were drawn again and pointed at my wolf.

"Give up, Shifter King," Malcolm cackled from his spot on the stairs. "You're surrounded. Shift back and they won't kill you all."

Ash secured Aurelia in his arms and glanced down at me. "You ready to mow them down?"

I nodded since it was the only way I could communicate in my wolf form. My wolf howled and jumped up from his crouch, crashing into the first row of agents. Guns went off, but Ash's magic prevented the bullets from hitting us.

He blew the bullets away on the breeze as another gust of wind pushed back the second row of agents. They fell like dominoes into each other, giving us a small window to escape.

"No!" Malcolm bellowed. "Get up, you fools. They're getting away!"

Men scrambled and a hand grasped my leg. I tripped over my paw and stepped on the man's chest. A crunch sounded beneath me, and the man screamed. My weight must have broken a rib, but his hand went slack, and I bounded away from him.

"Where are we going?" Dan asked through heaving breaths.

"We can't let them follow us back to the building. There are innocents there." Ash adjusted his hold on my mate.

"We need to get to the car so Grey can shift." Dan picked up his pace, jogging down a dark alley.

We'd known going into this that it could end up this way, so we'd had a back-up plan. We just needed to get to the SUV.

Stomping steps came from behind us, and my wolf growled low in my throat. They were following us. I'd known they would, but we had to move faster. I rammed my head into Asher's thigh and nudged him faster.

Dan opened a door at the end of the alley, and it creaked, the sound like a gunshot to my oversensitive ears. The humans were still pretty far away, so hopefully they wouldn't hear it.

I bounded into the dark room, which was likely a storage closet. The four of us barely fit inside the small space, but we weren't staying there long.

Dan closed the door quietly behind him and clicked the lock into place. The businesses in the alley had all been owned by shifters until we were outed to the world, and they had places that shifters or other supernaturals could go to hide if the need arose.

We'd always had a contingency plan... until the Fae Council came along and ruined everything. We had never planned for this madness.

Dan flicked on a light and threw a bundle of clothes at me. I shifted quickly and dressed to leave. We needed to get to our vehicle.

"There were agents following us. We need to get to the SUV. We can't risk everyone though." I ran a hand through my hair.

This was all so fucked. I reached for Aurelia, still unconscious in Ash's arms. The only way I knew she was alive was the faint beating of her heart.

"What the fuck happened?" I asked as I followed Dan out of a hidden door into what used to be a restaurant.

"Those knives the Fae had... they must have had something on them to prevent healing." Dan clicked the door shut behind him, and we followed him into the cool night air.

"We need to get her somewhere safe. She's lost too much blood." I pulled her closer to my chest.

Ash sighed. "The compound is heavily warded and there's no one there, with my brothers helping at the Syndicate."

"Okay, let's go." I gripped the door handle and pulled it open.

I jumped in the backseat with Aurelia curled in my lap. I pressed my lips to her forehead, praying that we could figure out a way to save her in time. I needed her. The entire supernatural world needed her.

"Fuck!" Dan yelled as a gunshot exploded in the air.

He dove in the driver's seat and slammed the door quickly behind him as bullets pinged the metal. My SUVs were all bulletproof, which was why I insisted we bring one of them instead of the mission-ready SUVs the Syndicate used.

"Drive!" I shouted as bullets pinged off the metal.

Dan sat up in his seat and pushed the button to start the vehicle and threw it into drive. We tore out of the abandoned parking lot as quickly as possible while men in suits chased after us, shooting the entire time.

"Take as many turns and side streets as you can before going into the woods east of Dallas," Ash instructed.

Dan tore down alley after alley, but it was taking too long to get where we needed to go. Aurelia's respiration was getting lighter the longer we took to get to the Rider's compound.

"We need to get there, now. I think we lost them." I pulled Aurelia's head on my shoulder, squeezing her tighter.

"Are you sure?" Dan asked and glanced at Ash.

"Yeah, I think Grey is right. We lost them, and the princess needs healing." Ash clenched his fist.

He glanced back at me holding her with a grimace. Dan's knuckles were white, he was gripping the steering wheel so tightly.

"There's just one problem. None of us are healers." Dan's eyes widened in the rearview mirror as he spoke.

"We'll worry about that when we get to the compound," Ash said, but he seemed scared himself.

My mate inspired loyalty in nearly everyone she met. The gods couldn't take her from me. She had to survive these wounds. She had to.

My wolf whimpered in my mind at the thought of losing his mate. His power was stronger than almost any other supernatural. If he lost his mate, I didn't know if I would be able to control him, or that I would even want to.

The world would burn if she died, and I would light the match.

Dan tore through the city streets and in no time, we were driving down a dirt road into the forest. The road was bumpy, and I shielded Aurelia from it as best as I could. She didn't open her eyes, but she was still breathing at least.

Ash pulled something from his pocket and hit a couple buttons when we got to the wrought iron gate that surrounded the compound. The gates creaked open too slowly for my liking, and I shifted in my seat.

This was taking too damn long. How much blood had Aurelia lost? We needed to get her inside and get a healer there. Dan hit the gas as soon as the gate opened, and followed the curved driveway to a state-of-the-art garage that was already open.

As soon as the SUV was parked, I threw my door open. "Get Fenrick on the phone immediately."

"Got it, boss." Dan pulled his phone from his pocket.

Ash ushered me through the door in the garage that led to the main house. I didn't even look at the place as I followed him down the long hallway. Dan was hot on our heels, barking orders into his phone.

"How's he going to get here?" Dan asked, as we turned a corner into a spare bedroom.

I laid Aurelia on the bed as Ash spoke. "The king has been here before. It was a very long time ago, but he should be able to sift to the gate."

I ran my fingers through Aurelia's hair as the two men spoke quietly in the corner about Fenrick. They would get him here. I knew they would. My wolf whined in my head to be let out, but I couldn't lose control right now.

After she's healed.

Once Fenrick arrived and healed her, I could shift and sleep by her side. I didn't want to be apart from her any more than my wolf did.

"Fenrick and the king will be here momentarily," Ash said.

I glanced up from my mate, noticing that Dan was gone, and Ash had pulled a chair up on the other side of the bed. I peered back at Aurelia, not wanting to take my eyes off her for another second.

Her heartbeat had slowed significantly, even though the bleeding had finally stopped.

"I think you need to get cleaned up, Grey." Ash grimaced.

I was covered in blood, but I couldn't bring myself to care. I wasn't leaving Aurelia's side until she was healed.

"No."

"Grey, you're covered in your mate's blood and the blood of the men you killed tonight," Ash said.

"I didn't kill anyone tonight. Besides, you're covered in blood too." I never took my eyes from Aurelia's pale face.

I leaned down and kissed her forehead, pushing every bit of love and devotion I had for her into the kiss.

"I know, and as soon as Dan gets back to make sure you don't shift and tear Fenrick apart when he heals Aurelia, I'm going to go clean up." Ash shook his head.

"I have no intention of hurting Fenrick," I huffed.

"I know you don't, but your wolf nearly maimed me earlier for getting close to the princess." He shook his hand out.

"You got too close to his injured mate. I calmed him down." I brushed the hair away from Aurelia's face. "What is taking so long?"

"We're here," Fenrick announced from the doorway.

He rushed inside the room and cursed when he inspected the wound in her stomach.

"It's not healing. I need you to heal her," I mumbled.

What if he couldn't heal her? Was I about to lose my mate no matter what?

"I'm going to try, Grey, but I need you to move." Fenrick patted my shoulder.

"I can't. I have to stay close." My hand tightened around hers.

Dan gripped my shoulder. "Move, Grey. She needs a healer or she's going to die. I will move you myself, if I have to."

He was right. I needed to move, but how could I force myself away from her when she was injured? My wolf howled in my mind and butted against my barriers as I stood. He didn't want to be too far from his mate.

I held my hands up in surrender and backed away from the bed. Every step away from her was painful. My heart cracked in my chest, but I stepped back all the same. I needed her to be okay. I needed it more than my next breath.

"Just fix her," I whispered.

My hands clenched into fists at my sides even as my wolf howled and whined and attempted to break free. I needed her healed.

There would be no world I wanted to live in if she died. I would incinerate it all, and every single person responsible for her death would pay.

Chapter 3
AURELIA

MY BODY BURNED on my left side. Why was I so hot? I threaded my fingers through soft fur. What? My eyes blinked open to a sterile white room and a black wolf asleep practically on top of me.

What the hell happened? Where are we?

The black wolf was obviously Grey, but what had happened to us? Nothing in the room was familiar. I sat up, wincing at the pain in my gut. Memories flooded back to me of the fight with the humans, and me being injured.

I ran my fingers over my abdomen where the blade had cut through my skin. It was no longer bleeding and there were no puckered scars from the serrated blade.

Did the Council actually capture us?

I shook the big wolf body next to me and tried to wake him, but he didn't budge. Did they do something to him? Was that why I couldn't get him to wake up? What was going on? This room wasn't the best, but it also didn't remind me of how the Council treated their prisoners.

"Grey," I croaked.

I needed water. It was like I'd chewed glass the night before and swallowed it. I nudged Grey again, and his wolf whined in his sleep but still didn't open his eyes.

"Grey, wake up. What happened?" I shoved his flank.

His wolfy tongue lolled out of his mouth, and in any other situation I would have found that adorable, but my hands were shaking, and my imagination was running wild with what the Council could have done to us to keep us here.

The wolf whimpered and turned blinking blue eyes at me before that same tongue licked up the side of my face with a yip of excitement.

"Hey, wolfie. I'm glad to see you too, but I need to talk to Grey." I buried my face in his fur, surreptitiously wiping the wolf drool off my face.

The wolf whined but seconds later, a very naked Grey pulled me into his arms. "You're alive."

"We have to find a way out of here. What happened? How did they catch us?" I asked rapid-fire.

I tugged out of his grip and grasped his hand in mine to pull him out of the bed, but he was immovable.

"Stop. We're safe, Aurelia. What are you talking about?" Grey frowned.

"Where are we then, Grey? I've never seen this place before." I chewed my lip.

"We couldn't go back to the building because we were being followed. This is the Riders' compound. We're safe." He kissed my temple. "I promise we're safe."

Safe? Are we really safe anywhere?

"The Riders' compound?" I asked, my heart cracking in my chest.

They had lost their brother because he was helping me, and now I was taking refuge in their space. How was that even fair? They had all done nothing but help us with this Fae Council problem and I was grateful to them for it, but now guilt gnawed at me.

"Hey, don't think like that. I can already see and smell the guilt all over you. Helping us helps all supernaturals, and Asher would be happy to help you heal." Grey wrapped his arms around my waist and pulled me into his naked body.

"How the hell can you smell my guilt?" I asked.

"I'm the Shifter King, mate. My nose is better than anyone's." He rested his chin on the top of my head.

"We're really safe and at the Riders' compound?" I asked.

I trusted Grey with my life, but I needed confirmation with everything that had happened. I just couldn't believe that they actually got us away from the President's Secret Service detail.

"Yes, but now I need to ask how you're feeling. You didn't heal. They stabbed you, and you weren't healing. It drove me and my wolf to madness thinking you were going to die."

"I'm fine." I turned my gaze up to him and kissed his chin.

There was a shadow of a beard there that tickled my nose and I giggled. I rested my head on his chest and listened to the sound of his heart thumping beneath my ear, steady and strong. He was solid. I could always rely on Grey. He was my mate.

His fingers trailed over the line where the knife had sliced my stomach, but there was nothing there. Only the memory of that wound still existed between us.

"Should we get dressed and figure out what our next steps are?" I asked.

Grey's arms tightened around me like he didn't want to let me go. I understood the sentiment because I would have been the same if the roles were reversed.

"Not yet," Grey said with a growl.

His wolf was riding him. His eyes glowed as the wolf lunged to the surface. I raked my fingers through his hair and nuzzled into his neck, pressing my lips to his skin.

"I think everyone wants to know I'm okay," I said.

"Fuck everyone else. I'm your mate and I'm not ready to give you up to the rest of the world yet," Grey growled.

It was so strange after all the years that I'd had no one, to knowing I had a mate and parents who loved me. I had friends who trusted me and needed me. I was out of my element.

Grey's arms tightened around me, and he sighed. "You're right. We need to go so they all know you're okay."

"We need to come up with a plan," I mumbled into his chest.

Things were getting worse now more than ever. Those agents' blank eyes flashed in my memory. They weren't normal. Malcolm had been controlling them, and if we didn't do something about it, we were in a lot more trouble than we'd bargained for.

"You should probably get dressed first." I giggled.

Grey glanced down at his naked body, which drew my own gaze. Did I really want him to get dressed? All that tanned, toned skin was on display. I shifted next to him and winced in pain. I was still stiff and sore, even though someone had healed me.

Grey pushed me back to the bed and got up, grabbing a pair of sweats from the chair next to the bed. "You're still sore."

"Only a little." I pouted.

"Come on, let's go tell the others you're awake, and figure out how we're going to stop the Council." Grey held a hand out to me.

I glowered but gingerly got up from the bed. Someone had changed me into sleep shorts and a tank. Pretty sure it was Grey, I squeezed his hands in thanks. I didn't want anyone else changing my clothes. I didn't care who it was.

Grey opened the door, and Fenrick fell inside from his sitting position on the floor. He blinked his eyes open rapidly and jumped to his feet.

"What's going on?" Fenrick scanned the hallway.

His shoulders bunched and his hands clenched into fists at his sides as he searched for a threat.

"Everything's fine." I smiled at Fenrick.

His eyes widened and he blew out a relieved breath. "You scared us, Princess."

"I kind of scared myself." I chuckled.

"Never again," Grey growled.

"None of us can promise that. All we can do is our best not to let it happen again, and I promise to do *my* best so it doesn't." I stepped forward. "Now, we need to come up with a plan."

"You're right, Princess," Fenrick muttered as he led the way down the hall. "I picked up Zeke's laptop before I came to help heal you."

I hung my head and a single tear leaked from my eye. Zeke. He'd been shot, and I'd left him behind. Grey squeezed my hip as he felt my guilt over the loss of the Rider.

What would Ash think of me? It was my fault that his brother was gone.

"It's not your fault, mate." Grey squeezed me again.

"Isn't it, though? That was my plan. I'd wanted to take Malcolm out, and then we couldn't even find him." I shook my head.

"You can't blame yourself, Aurelia. We made you leave him behind. It's what he would have wanted." Grey pulled me down the hall.

"Are you absolutely sure about that? I hate that we had to leave him, but you all made sure that even though I was injured to the point of death, you brought me back and healed me. My life isn't worth more than anyone else's."

Fenrick turned sharply and scowled at me. "It's not? You are the one prophesized to save the supernaturals and usher in a new era. How can you say your life isn't worth more? You are meant to rule and save us all."

"Why?" I threw my hands up in frustration. "Because some seer two hundred years ago said it was true? I haven't done anything but screw up and get people I care about killed."

Both men stared at me with equal expressions of disbelief. What were they thinking? I hadn't saved anyone. Zeke had died because he was protecting us.

"You have ordered the people at the syndicate to rescue the supernaturals being targeted by the government, have you not?" Fenrick asked slowly.

"It's the right thing to do." I crossed my arms over my chest. They were innocents and didn't deserve to be persecuted. I was right to help them.

"You helped destroy a prison that innocent supernaturals were being held at and destroyed much of the Council's research into mind control."

Fenrick had a point, but I still wasn't sure what it was. "That was selfish. I needed Grey and the rest of you back. I needed my family.

The others that were released? I don't even know if they were innocent or not." I glared at him.

"We were all innocent in that we didn't commit the crimes of which they accused us. There weren't any crimes, really. Simply existing is the crime they accused you of as well." Fenrick crossed his arms over his chest.

"I know. I just don't think I've done all that much to inspire this kind of loyalty. We need to get a plan together to get rid of the Council once and for all." I stepped past Fenrick to the door behind him.

People were whispering on the other side, and my shoulders slumped as I recognized Ash's voice. Did he hate me? How could I even face him when I'd let his brother die?

I squared my shoulders and pushed through the door. My father was the first to glance up at me, and he was on his feet before I could even take a step into the room. His arms wrapped around me, and he blew out a relieved breath.

"I'm so glad you're okay, daughter," he said.

"I'm not exactly sure I am. What information do we have that can help eliminate the Council and stop the humans?" My voice was robotic even to my own ears.

"We know where one of the facilities are where they are holding supernaturals. We could rescue them, so they can help us in the coming war," Fenrick spoke up.

"How?" I asked.

"Zeke was searching for them." Fenrick hung his head.

He must have heard what happened to Zeke. A tear dropped down my cheek, and I nodded for him to continue. My throat burned with grief, and if I tried to talk, it would have been unrecognizable.

"He found one that we could probably infiltrate and get people out of there."

"Well, Zeke was searching for these places to help people. Given that he's gone now, I think he would want us to go after them. Let's make a plan and free our people," I said with a conviction I didn't feel.

We were going to save the supernaturals, and then we were going to destroy the Council. Zeke deserved that from us.

Chapter 4

GREY

I PULLED Aurelia against my chest. It was late in the evening after strategizing all day to infiltrate the facility. "We need to rest and recharge."

"I don't want to wait to save them," Aurelia said but yawned.

"You almost died less than a day ago. You need sleep and I need to hold you," I whispered.

The others in the room clearly heard me but none of them acknowledged our conversation.

Dan cleared his throat. "I need to make some calls and get supplies. I think it's best we wait until tomorrow night."

Aurelia leaned forward, but my arms tightened around her. I wasn't letting her off my lap. She turned her glare on me and wiggled her hips. If she really thought that was going to be an incentive for me to let her up, she was wrong.

"Stop it, mate," I growled in her ear. "Rest is going to be the last thing on my mind if you keep that up."

Her breath caught in her throat as I squeezed her thigh, holding her down on my hard cock. I was always hard when she was near me, but with her wiggling in my lap, it was even worse. I needed to show her how much I needed her.

She'd almost died, and then all we've been doing since was planning this break-in. I needed to prove to myself that she was still here. She wasn't dead.

"Fine." She huffed. "We can go in tomorrow night and rescue them."

I stood in one fluid motion and tossed my mate over my shoulder, who squeaked in surprise and slapped my ass.

"Grey, I can walk." She batted at my back.

I nipped her ass cheek playfully and continued out of the room to the sound of muffled laughter from the others.

I didn't give a fuck. I needed my mate. *Now.* I raced through the hall to the room that Asher had given us and kicked the door shut before tossing her on the bed.

"Grey, what are you doing? I thought you wanted to rest." She leaned back on her elbows.

"There's plenty of time for that."

I pulled the T-shirt off over my head with one hand and smirked as her gaze followed my movements. She was so fucking perfect, and she was all mine.

She sat up on her knees before me and reached for the button on my jeans. I batted her hands away and wrapped her wrists in one of my hands behind her back.

My wolf howled and battled to the surface at the knowledge that we had our mate at our mercy. My hands shifted to claws, but I was careful not to let the one around her wrists scratch her skin.

"Grey?" She peered into my eyes. "These don't belong to me."

I traced the back of my claw along her collarbone to the thin strap of material holding the tiny tank top on her body. "I'll buy them new ones."

I snapped both straps quickly and leaned over, licking a path down her neck to her shoulder, to the place I planned to mark her fully as mine. I nipped the skin there, and Aurelia moaned.

Her tiny tank pooled around her waist, showing off her beautiful breasts.

"I want to touch you too." She struggled in my grip to no avail.

I wasn't letting her go. I would never let her go again. "Lean back and grab the headboard. If you're a good girl, I'll let you touch me all you want, mate."

Her eyes lit up with my words, and I released her wrists. Aurelia pulled the ruined tank top off along with the small sleep shorts and laid back on the bed, gripping the headboard.

"Fuck, you're perfect, mate." I leaned over her and took her nipple into my mouth, swirling my tongue around it before nipping it.

Aurelia's back arched but she didn't let go of the headboard as I stared up into her eyes that were blazing with need.

I plucked at her other nipple with my fingers as I kissed my way to it. I sucked the nipple into my mouth and gave it the same treatment.

"Grey, I need you." Aurelia panted and squirmed beneath me, seeking that friction.

Her hips bucked up to meet mine, but I was still wearing my jeans. "Patience, my love. You're such a good girl. I want to reward you."

My tongue darted out, licking my way down her body to the spot she needed me most. I gripped her inner thigh, rubbing my thumb across all her creamy skin as I pushed her legs as far open as they would go.

"I'm going to fuck you with my tongue until you're dripping wet for me," I murmured against her stomach. "You're going to be so mindless for me, but you won't take your hands off the headboard will you, my good girl?"

She shook her head but didn't answer with words. "I need you to tell me you won't let go."

"I won't let go. Please," she begged.

"Please what? What do you need, mate?"

"I need you, Grey. I need my mate." She was breathless.

I growled against her stomach, my cock going harder than I ever thought possible. She'd called me her mate in that breathy tone, and my wolf surged to the surface again. I barely held him back from taking over and biting her, making her mine entirely.

I blew out a breath and locked the wolf down before running my finger up her dripping wet pussy. "You're already so wet for me."

"Yes, Grey," she moaned.

I pushed a single finger inside her and curled it in a way I knew would have her climbing in seconds. She arched back and her head thrashed as I pumped my finger inside her pussy. I added a second and circled her clit with my thumb.

"Grey, oh gods!" Aurelia screamed as convulsions wracked through her body.

Her walls tightened around my fingers almost painfully as she spasmed with her first orgasm. I stroked her inner thigh as I waited for her to come down. I needed to taste her, needed to feel her wrapped around my cock. My cock throbbed, begging for attention.

I glanced up at Aurelia with a grin to see she was still holding on to the headboard with a white-knuckle grip. Her breaths came out in shallow pants as she squirmed.

"Grey, I need to touch you." She pouted.

"Not yet, my love." I leaned in and lapped at her juices.

She groaned low in her throat and wiggled her hips, still needy even after her first orgasm, and I loved that about her. She was never satisfied until my cock was inside her. My tongue circled her overstimulated clit, and she screamed.

Fuck, her noises and screams were everything. I sucked her button into my mouth, and her thighs locked around my head, holding me where she needed me as her second orgasm blasted through her and she screamed my name.

I chuckled against her clit, the vibration only prolonging her euphoria as she clenched her thighs harder. Her juices gushed out in a wave, and I lapped at every single drop before her thighs went slack and she growled.

"Fuck me, mate," she commanded, and it was the sexiest thing I'd heard in my life.

I sat up and moved off the bed, tearing at the buttons on my jeans. I needed them off, needed inside her. She sat up on her knees and clenched her hands repeatedly before reaching for my open jeans and gripping me through my boxers.

"Fuck, Aurelia. I don't know if I can handle you touching me right now."

"Too bad." She leaned in, kissing me hard and tasting her own juices on my tongue as she rubbed my cock lightly.

Her other hand ran down my shoulder, over my chest, and I shuddered under her touch. "What are you doing to me?" I groaned.

She squeezed my cock and grinned. Aurelia kissed down my neck to my shoulder, nipping it lightly before moving further. My knees buckled, and I twisted to fall back on the bed pulling her down on top of me.

"I'm going to slowly torture you the way you did me." She took my nipple between her teeth and smirked.

Pain mixed with the pleasure of her slowly running her fingers over my still clothed cock. She kissed, nipped and sucked her way down to the waistband of my jeans, and I sucked in a sharp breath when she reached inside my boxers and shoved them down so my cock sprang free.

"Aurelia, stop," I said with no conviction. "If you put your mouth on me, I'm not going to last. You're too perfect."

She didn't listen and ran her tongue up the underside of my shaft before swirling it around the head. I shouted her name and gripped her under her arms, pulling her up my body.

I kissed her hard and rubbed my aching cock along her slit. Her hips bucked, and a soft moan left her lips.

"If you want to be in charge, you can, but you're going to ride my cock." I pushed her down on my dick, all the way to the hilt.

She tilted her head back, and her long hair tickled my thighs as she squeezed her eyes closed and just felt the connection between us. I hadn't realized how much I needed this until that moment.

My cock twitched inside of her as she held still, and I adjusted my hips to hit that spot inside her with the tip. She circled her hips before sitting back and bouncing up and down a couple times. It was fucking heaven.

"I'm so full, Grey. Fuck, it feels so good." She circled her hips again, but I needed her to move.

I gripped her hips and lifted her off me almost to the point I was no longer inside her and then slammed her body back down, both of us screaming. Aurelia dug her nails into my chest, leaving crescent-shaped marks on my chest.

She could mark me as often as she wanted. I was hers.

I lifted her over and over again as she rocked her hips back to mine until tingles started at my balls and ran up my spine. I thrust my hips up into her wildly as my impending orgasm shook me to my core.

At the last second, I flipped us in one fluid motion and threaded my fingers through hers on either side of her head. I fucked her hard and fast as my balls drew up and a roar exploded from my lips as I came harder than I ever had before.

I leaned down and kissed her with a savageness I had never felt before and collapsed on top of her before rolling to the side and pulling her into my arms. Aurelia's eyes glowed with love as she stared up at me with her chin on my chest.

"I think that was exactly what we needed," I whispered and kissed her forehead. "We need to remember what's important. What we are fighting for."

"What if I've forgotten what that is?" she asked, glancing away.

I gripped her chin and turned her back to face me. "What do you think we're fighting for?"

"Right now, it feels a lot like vengeance," she said.

"We aren't fighting for vengeance. We're fighting for the right to live and be free. To love who we want without persecution, and we will defeat the Council because they are fighting for greed, but our lives literally depend on it."

Chapter 5
AURELIA

I WAS FIDGETING. I knew it, and everyone else did too. Grey wrapped his hand around both of mine to stop me.

"The last break-in didn't go so well," I mumbled.

"The plans got changed last time. No one here is going to change the plans." Grey squeezed my hand.

"A million things could go wrong." I chewed my bottom lip.

"It could also go smoothly. You must have faith that we are exactly where we need to be." He leaned back in the driver's seat of his SUV as we waited for the signal.

"What about Dan and Fenrick? They have to set it off."

Ash patted my shoulder from the back seat. "Stop worrying, Princess. They're both skilled warriors. They won't fail you."

He said it like they were doing this just for me and not the good of all supernaturals, and I didn't know how I felt about that. I didn't want them to fail, but they wouldn't be failing me if they did. We were here for everyone, not just a few.

Grey tensed, and I turned to him just as the explosion rattled the windows of the SUV. Fire and smoke rose behind the building we were watching, and I shoved open the door. We all scrambled from the vehicle as Fenrick appeared in front of us with a grin.

"Time to go." He placed a hand on my shoulder, the other on Grey's and sifted us into the building.

I stumbled slightly and Grey's hand on my arm steadied me as we appeared in a dark room. Dan stood in front of us, his gaze far off as he stared at something I couldn't see.

"Dan?" I asked.

He spun around, his eyes wide, and I gasped at the glimpse I got from behind him.

"No," I said.

"What?" Grey asked.

He marched forward to peer around Dan. "Fuck. What are they doing?"

The scene before me was like something out of a horror movie. The window Dan stood in front of was like a viewing window. Ultraviolet lights glowed in the room beyond.

Beds lined the walls and supernaturals were unconscious with tubes coming out of them. IV bags pumped a bright blue liquid into their veins.

"What is going on? Is this a testing facility?" I asked in shock.

"It is, but I never even imagined it would be like this, though. They're killing them," Fenrick growled.

"This is crazy. How are we supposed to get everyone out when they're hooked up to tubes?" I planted my hands on my hips and hung my head.

We didn't think this through. How could we do anything to rescue these people when we didn't have enough help?

"The facility is huge. Maybe the Shadow Warriors are in a different section." Fenrick patted my shoulder.

"They're all shifters," Grey said, sniffing the air. "They aren't going to last much longer. We need to get them out now."

I squeezed Grey's hand in comfort. He could feel their torment as the Shifter King and their ultimate Alpha. This had to be the hardest on him.

"Fenrick, can you go sift and get my parents? We need as many Fae that are on our side to sift these people out." I glanced at my childhood protector.

Fenrick nodded and sifted from the room. Something wasn't sitting right with me. How were we able to sift in and out at all, let alone undetected?

"Is the Council getting sloppy?" I wondered.

"Why would you think that?" Grey asked.

"Does this seem too easy to you? We sifted in undetected."

"Maybe they think the human government got to us first?" Grey folded his arms over his chest.

Fenrick popped back in a minute later with both my parents and the Shadow Guardian that helped me get out of Faery when I was trapped there. I sighed in relief. They were here to help get those people out of there.

I rushed to the door next to the viewing window and wrenched it open, but a siren blared as soon as I stepped through the door. "Fuck. We need to get them out of here immediately."

My parents and the Guardian jumped into action, unhooking the shifters as quickly as possible and sifting several of them out at once.

"C'mon." Grey gripped my hand and dragged me through another door at the other end of the room.

This room was more of the same, and I deflated. We had our work cut out for us. How on earth were we going to get everyone out of here with the sirens blaring and guards most likely baring down on us?

I spun in a circle, searching for someone who could help us get some of the people out. A man sat up in a bed at the other end of the room. His eyes glimmered with hope as he stared at me.

"Grey, the Fae are in this room." I ran to the man and pulled the wires from his arms and unbuckled the straps around his wrists and ankles. "Can you walk?"

"Princess Aurelia, I knew you would come." The man bowed his head to me.

"Less bowing and more getting the fuck out of here," I grumbled, still hating the bowing and scraping thing.

Grey chuckled. "She doesn't like that. We also don't have a lot of time. Is everyone here Fae?"

"Yes. Mostly guards from the Shadow Kingdom who refused to

fall in line." The man jumped from the cot and stumbled slightly, holding his head.

"Easy. You've been tied to that bed for a while, I'm guessing." Grey reached out and gripped his arm.

"I've been here for a long time," the man grumbled. "I just need a second."

"We may not have a second. Can you sift?" I glanced back at the door.

The sirens continued to wail, and I scanned the room. I glanced at the ceiling and groaned. In each corner was a dome with a blinking red light on it. They were recording everything that happened in the room.

"We're being watched. They're probably waiting to ambush us any second." I straightened my spine.

Grey rushed over to another gurney where another man was struggling and helped remove the tubes from his body. The man stood quickly, and the two of them went to work on the rest of the men in the room.

"We need to keep moving, or there's no way we'll get everyone out of here." Grey said, reaching for my arm.

We moved through the room to another door but this one was locked. I shoved against it, but it wouldn't budge.

"Step back," I said to Grey.

I let a small trickle of magic fill my palm and flung it at the door. A deafening boom filled the space as Grey launched himself at me, tackling me to the floor. Debris sailed over our heads and smoke billowed from the now open doorway.

"We could have thought of a better way, Aurelia," Grey chided.

"We don't have time for all that," I grunted beneath him.

His big shifter body was heavy. He rolled to the side and hopped to his feet, reaching a hand down to me as Dan pushed through the main door with his eyes wild.

"What happened?" Dan stared at the burning rubble that was once a door.

"That was me." I grinned.

Grey grabbed the fire extinguisher and blasted the door with it until the flames died, and we could walk into the next room. More beds sat in the room with supernaturals lying in them. How many people did this awful place have?

The door at the other end of the room flew open, and men flooded through it one by one. I backed up into Grey and turned to him, but his eyes were widened at the door we'd just come through.

More Council soldiers were blocking the exit and we weren't any closer to getting the others out. There had to be hundreds of beds in this room. It was ten times larger than the others.

"What are we going to do?" I asked. "None of us can sift."

I would be able to sift eventually, but I had yet to learn how. Was this the time to experiment? Probably not, but if we couldn't figure something else out before we were captured, then I would have to try and pray to the gods it worked.

The guards filed in with batons in their hands lit up with electricity. Fenrick popped in and cursed before gripping onto two of the gurneys and sifting out again.

We were on our own. Fuck, we were in so much trouble. What the hell were we going to do? I pooled magic in my palms and scanned the crowd of about twenty guards. There were only three of us, so the odds were stacked against us.

"You need to try to sift back, Aurelia." Grey grabbed my arm and turned me to face him.

"I can't." I shook my head.

The man across from me smirked, and I recognized him as one of the men who'd captured us outside the prison. He wasn't the asshole who'd wanted me as a toy, but he was just as bad. From what I'd heard, Grey killed the man who tried to own me.

I wasn't losing sleep over that. He'd deserved to die for his crimes. I just wished I could have been there to see it. Maybe I was becoming a little bloodthirsty when it came to the Council. Oh, well.

More magic pooled in my hands as I gazed around the room at all the supernaturals they were keeping in stasis. They were performing testing on them. Probably their mind control, but how was I supposed to get them out of there when I couldn't sift? Dan and Grey couldn't either. We were completely stuck.

"Give yourselves up and no one gets hurt!" the Fae guard roared.

The others fanned out around him and held up their batons. There was nowhere to go. Power buzzed beneath my skin as I held my ground. The guard smirked like he knew it wasn't going to be that easy.

It wasn't. I couldn't let it be easy for them. If they were going to catch me, they were going to have to work for it. Shadows writhed around my arms as more magic than I have ever used before built inside me, buzzing like angry bees.

The men attacked as one just as blinding light mixed with shadows shot from my palms. The guards screamed and ducked, but it was too late. Every one of them was burned to ash in seconds.

Frantically, I turned to Grey and Dan, but they were fine. I breathed a sigh of relief, but the magic inside me was like a living thing. It knew we wouldn't actually be safe until we got everyone out of here.

I closed my eyes tight and imagined the infirmary in the syndicate. I needed everyone out of this building and healing.

Magic shot from me, and I swirled into time and space as I actually sifted for the first time. I stumbled as my feet hit solid ground, and strong arms wrapped around me.

"You are truly incredible, Aurelia," Grey said, squeezing me to him.

His eyes weren't on me, though. They were on the hundred men that had been in beds in that facility. I slumped into Grey's chest, but the relief was short-lived as exhaustion took over.

If Grey hadn't been holding me, I would have slumped to the ground and passed out. I passed out in his arms instead.

Chapter 6
GREY

"A HUNDRED WARRIORS ARE GREAT." I ran a hand down my face. "But they still won't be enough."

Aurelia was sleeping in my lap from her overuse of magic. Fenrick checked her to make sure she wasn't in distress or injured. I was thankful for the Guardian. He cared about her almost as much as I did.

"They won't be well enough to march into battle for a couple days anyway," Fenrick said.

"What are we going to do? The Council soldiers still outnumber us."

Dan tapped his index finger on the golden book. "Did Aurelia find anything that could help get rid of them yet?"

My mate stirred in my arms and sighed before laying her head back on my shoulder.

"Not yet. She's been looking but hasn't found anything concrete." I shifted her so she was more comfortable.

Aurelia's body stiffened and she shot up in my lap, nearly headbutting my chin. "Where are they? Did we get them all out?"

"Easy, love. They're in the infirmary, recovering." I rubbed her back in soothing circles. "You got everyone out and turned the guards to ash."

Her shoulders slumped, and I wasn't sure if it was from relief or guilt for killing the guards. It was probably a bit of both, I suspected.

"What were you just discussing?" Aurelia yawned.

She was still exhausted, and I hated that she wouldn't take the time for a proper rest after expending so much magic. I didn't even suggest it because I already knew what her answer would be.

"Even with the Shadow Warriors recovered from the facility, we don't have the manpower to take on the Council. We need more help." I squeezed her hip.

"Shit. What do we do? We could break into the other facilities, but those people aren't warriors. They're civilians." She tapped my hand and moved to stand, but I held her in my lap.

"We need a plan. We need more help."

A knock sounded on the door to the office, and I called out for whoever to come in. Everyone knew not to disturb us unless it was important, and by the scent from the other side of the door, I had to guess it was Magna with some kind of vision.

Sure enough, Magna pushed through the door a second later with a glint in her eye. "I've got a possible solution but it's not going to be easy."

"When is anything ever easy?" I asked.

"Do you want to know the solution, or are you going to just snark at me?" Magna raised a brow.

"Sorry, yes. What's the plan?"

"There is a group of rebels in Faery. Their numbers are growing every day. With the rebels' help, we will have enough people to take down the Council." Magna sat heavily in the chair from which Dan had stood.

Dan ran a hand through his hair. "You want us to go to Faery?"

"The two of us are needed here." Magna shook her head. "You need to work with our little army some more to get them ready."

"Who do you see going to Faery?" Aurelia asked, sitting up straighter.

I wished like hell that she would stay behind where it was the safest, but I knew that would never happen. My strong-willed mate would never let us go off into danger and leave her behind.

"Your father must go, so that means that Fenrick will volunteer as well. The two of you must go, so Asher will likely volunteer to go also," Magna said knowingly.

She wasn't wrong. Ash had become attached to Aurelia. He protected her just like Zeke had. I'd never seen the Riders of the Hunt actually care about something other than their bikes and each other, but they cared about the princess.

Ash crossed his arms over his chest. "You would be right about that. I'm not letting the princess go back into enemy territory without me again."

"It turned out just fine last time, Ash." Aurelia grinned.

"You were lucky last time. This time, you'll be protected at all costs." He glared down at her.

"I don't need a babysitter, but fine. If Magna says that she sees us all going together, I won't stop anyone from coming with us."

"Everyone go and grab what you need. Not more than you can carry. We will likely need to change into Fae clothes once we're there to blend anyway." I squeezed Aurelia and helped her stand.

We were going back to Faery. What could go wrong?

We didn't need to grab clothes, and Aurelia was a weapon in her own right, but I still grabbed a dagger and a weapon belt for her to wear while we were in Faery. Everyone there had magic, so having additional protection wouldn't hurt.

"Do I really need this?" Aurelia asked as I clipped the belt around her waist.

"Better to have it and not need it than need it and not have it." I shrugged.

The others met us in the garage not long after I got her situated. "Are we ready to go?"

They all nodded.

We raced out past the wards and Aurelia frowned. "How did I sift us into the building?"

"I don't know." I squeezed her shoulder. "I guess you're more powerful than the wards."

"That's slightly terrifying." She groaned.

"Why?" Ash asked next to me. "It's a good thing you're powerful enough to take care of yourself."

"Power corrupts. Look at the Council. I don't want to be corrupted like them." She shook her head.

"Just the fact that you're worried about it tells me something, mate." I glanced at her drawn features.

"What does it tell you?" she asked.

"That you could never be corrupted," Ash answered before I could.

I glared at him. That was my line. She could never be corrupt like the Council. She was too pure, and the fact was that she was worrying about having too much power for good and honest reasons proved it.

"He's right, my love. I was just going to say that before he interrupted me."

"Are you sure?" Her expression was skeptical.

"Absolutely," I said as I crossed the wards.

Aurelia didn't shudder like she usually did when she passed through them. She frowned in confusion. It made sense that if she was stronger than the magic holding the wards in place that she wouldn't feel the effects of walking through them.

Fenrick set a hand on my shoulder and his other on Aurelia's while the king placed his on Ash. We needed to get to Faery and try to recruit the rebels to our cause.

I swirled through time and space as we sifted to Faery once again. I breathed out a sigh when we landed in the forest outside the Shadow Kingdom.

"There's a small village close by where we can get information," Fenrick said.

"Let's go." Aurelia waved a hand for him to lead the way.

We picked through the forest around the brush, Aurelia occasionally laying her hand on a tree, smiling softly as it spoke to her. When we were just inside the tree line, she stopped and frowned.

"Something isn't right. The trees want us to stop and go the other direction."

"Why?" I asked.

"Danger." She shook her head. "All they know is that the town is dangerous to us."

"Should I glamour myself and take a look?" Fenrick asked.

"They don't like that idea either, but it's worth a shot." Aurelia tilted her head to the side as if she were listening to them.

"I'll go with you," I said. "If you can glamour me too."

"I can do that. Princess, stay here with Asher and your father. We'll be right back." Fenrick stared at Aurelia, probably waiting for her to argue.

"Fine. As long as no one goes alone."

Fenrick's eyes widened in shock that she didn't argue but the expression was quickly replaced with determination. The Guardian turned his stare on me, and magic tingled along my skin for a second.

"Is it done?" I asked.

My voice was lower and rougher than I'd ever heard it. I had no idea he could change the pitch of my voice along with my appearance.

"It's done. Let's go see what we can find." Fenrick stormed across the tree line.

I jogged up next to him and crossed my arms over my chest. What were we even looking for in that tiny town? I doubted the rebels would have their base in such a small place.

Fenrick squared his shoulders and marched to the place like he was still a soldier working for the king. Having that kind of attitude in unknown territory could be dangerous if he wasn't careful. We needed to blend in with the locals, not give them a reason to turn us over to the Council.

"Shit," I cursed.

Fenrick turned to me with a frown as I pointed at a sign in the town square. Wanted posters were plastered all over the town message board. I strolled up to the board as casually as I could while dread coursed through my body.

"What is that?" Fenrick whispered as he glanced at the board as well.

"Wanted posters. They have rewards out for us even here," I mumbled.

There was a picture of me that must have been taken when I was at the prison without my knowledge, and one of Fenrick and the king as well. Aurelia's picture was hand drawn and looked like it could be anyone.

"Can you read what that says?" I asked.

"Basically, if any of those people are spotted in Faery, they are to be turned over to the Council guards immediately. The reward is no taxes for a year." Fenrick clenched a fist.

"What do you mean, no taxes? I didn't think the kingdoms believed in taxation. They had enough land to be powerful and employed the common Fae to tend to it."

Was this the Council's doing? Were they taxing the citizens of Faery to keep them weak and the Council in control?

"The king never taxed his people. I don't know what this means, but we need to find out and stop it." Fenrick spun on his heel and stomped back to the tree line.

I followed close behind him, fuming. How could the Council start taxing their people when they'd never been taxed before? It was disgusting and then to add insult to injury, the reward for turning us in was going back to their normal way of life for a year.

We burst through the trees. Ash tensed, stepping in front of Aurelia before he realized it was us in glamour, and relaxed.

"The Council is even more corrupt than we realized, your Majesty." Fenrick hung his head.

"What?" the Shadow King asked.

"They are *taxing* the citizens of the Shadow Kingdom," Fenrick growled.

"Taxing?" Aurelia questioned. "Don't taxes keep a kingdom running?"

"No, my love. That's just what the humans say. The Fae don't tax their people. They help keep their people fed by employing them to tend the land and giving them options. This is disgusting."

"Also," Fenrick said. "They have a bounty on all our heads. The most desperate will try to hand us over to the Council."

"What's the bounty?" Ash asked, folding his arms over his chest.

"One year of no taxes," I growled.

"So, we basically need to act as if everyone in this realm is an enemy, or we could get captured by the Council?" Aurelia chewed her lip.

"This development just made our lives a hundred times harder." Fenrick scrubbed a hand down his face.

"Everyone needs to be glamoured, and no one goes anywhere alone. We all need to be on our toes. Desperate people do desperate things, and we don't want to be casualties," I said with a huff.

This was fucking bad. How were we going to find the rebels while dodging desperate Fae?

Chapter 7
AURELIA

"WE STILL NEED to go into town. What if the rebels are there and we miss them?" I shuffled my feet.

We couldn't just skip the town because there were signs up asking for information on us and putting bounties on our heads. We needed information, no matter how dangerous it was to obtain.

"I doubt the rebels made this tiny village their base of operations." Grey peered around the forest.

"They most likely didn't, but shouldn't we at least check it out before making assumptions? That will save us time." I crossed my arms over my chest.

"Okay, but we all need to be glamoured. Desperate people do desperate things, and they can't even be held responsible for those actions." Grey ran a hand down his face.

"That, I can do." I grinned.

I had been glamouring my wings for as long as I could remember. How hard could it be to change my appearance?

I closed my eyes and let a trickle of magic pour from my core to my limbs. I imagined red hair and brown eyes over my actual blonde hair and blue eyes. When I opened my eyes, everyone's shocked expressions met mine.

"Very good, daughter." My father nodded.

"You look completely different." Grey grinned.

"What about Ash?" I asked. "He's not Fae. How is he going to blend in?"

"I'll glamour him," Father said, turning to Asher. "If he will allow me to."

"Of course, Your Majesty." Ash nodded.

It was the first time I'd ever heard the Rider show deference to my father as the Shadow King. He called me Princess all the time, but I didn't remember him ever addressing my father that way.

I glanced between the two of them with a shrug. Grey wrapped an arm around me, and we picked our way through the underbrush and crossed the tree line into the little village.

"This is mainly people who worked the fields for the palace," Father said.

"And now they are doing what?" I asked.

"I don't know. If the Council is taxing them, then they are basically slaves." He clenched his hands into fists.

"They need to be stopped," I whispered.

We strolled through the town, peering around at the drawn faces. That wasn't what I remembered of the small village.

It had always been lively, with smiling Fae and friendliness. Everyone glared at each other with suspicion.

What had happened to them? Was the Council really using them as slaves?

As we walked through the town whispers followed us. The gazes of the townspeople were distrusting and accusatory.

"Shit," my father said behind me, and I turned my shocked gaze on him.

"What?" I asked.

He nodded to a man standing in a nearby doorway. "Thomas can see through glamour."

"My King," the man mumbled. "How could you abandon us?"

My father's shoulders slumped at the accusation. "I didn't abandon you. Hold out hope we are going to fix everything."

"There is no hope left. They are making us work your fields and giving us just enough to sustain one person, even those who have families. Everything else they take for their army. They take *everything*."

"We are going to stop them." I stepped toward Thomas.

"I'm sorry, my King, but I have to feed my family." Thomas glanced away.

"What are you talking about?" I asked.

Thomas made a hand motion and suddenly we were surrounded by Council guards. "Forgive me."

My father nodded to the man. Swords were drawn all around us, but there was something off with these guards. Their eyes were blank, just like the human Secret Service agents.

"I thought Fae had shields around their minds?" I asked, glancing between my father and Fenrick.

"They do," Fenrick said, stepping up to my side.

"Then how are they being controlled?" Magic pooled in my palms as the guards rushed forward.

Ash used his elemental magic to push them back, but it didn't work for long. There were ten of them and only five of us. We'd survived worse odds before, but we'd always been in the human realm.

Everyone in the village had magic and would do whatever they could to capture us to feed their families. Desperation grew thick in the air. The promise of no taxes and more food was too tempting for people who had been starving.

"What do you mean, they are being controlled?" my father asked.

"Their eyes are just like the Secret Service agents." I threw a small ball of magic at the encroaching guards.

They dove out of the way before the magic could hit them.

Grey slid in front of me and growled. "We can't worry about that. We need to get out of here."

"We've drawn a crowd." Fenrick grimaced.

I glanced over my shoulder to find angry Fae staring at us like they wanted to kill us all. Well, that was just great. What were we going to do now that we were surrounded by even more enemies?

"I don't want to hurt them," I sighed. "They're just desperate Fae that need help."

"We can't help them if the Council gets their hands on you." Fenrick clapped a hand on my shoulder.

"I don't know how much longer I can hold them off, Princess," Ash grunted.

"We're going to have to fight our way out, Aurelia. It's the only way," Grey said over his shoulder.

My shadows pulsed and writhed along my arms as I allowed magic to pool in my palms. I couldn't help but wonder what might happen if the guards were no longer under the control of the Council. Would they be on our side, or would they still come after us?

"Let them come, Ash. We aren't getting out of here any faster this way," I said.

Ash dropped the magic, and the guards rushed forward. Grey pulled the sword from his side and rushed the nearest guards. They all formed a circle around me, swords drawn and battling with the Council guards.

The magic pulsed in my hands and my shadows writhed down my arms, mixing together in a huge ball of sparkling shadow. I blinked down at the magic, unsure if I should use it. What was it going to do to the Fae around me?

The memory of my shadows and magic melting the skin off one of the guards assaulted me and I grimaced. No. I didn't want my magic to do that. I wanted it to help these people.

With my intentions clear, magic shot out of my body in every direction. It blasted every enemy to the ground, but my friends remained standing. I stumbled and covered my eyes, praying I hadn't just made a terrible mistake and incinerated the entire village.

I could never live with myself if I had hurt all the innocent people in this place. I covered my face with my hands, not daring to look at the possible carnage, but screams never came.

Someone grabbed my hands. I'd recognize Grey's presence anywhere. He pulled my hands away from my face and grinned.

"What did you just do?" he asked.

He was standing directly in front of me, so I couldn't glimpse the carnage.

"Are they all dead?" I choked out.

A groan met my ears and then another and another. What the hell had I done? Were they all dying slow deaths? I moved to the side and glanced over Grey's shoulder. The guards were all blinking and holding their heads.

"What happened?" one of them asked. "My head's all fuzzy."

I blinked at the Fae man. His eyes were no longer blank, they were confused. Had I actually lifted their mind control?

I dropped my glamour and stood directly in front of him. "Do you know who I am?"

He instantly dropped his face to the ground in a deep bow that the rest of the guards all followed. "Your Highness. What's happened? They told us you were dead."

"They had you under mind control." I shook my head and motioned for them all to rise.

"I remember now. They put us in prison for refusing to join their ranks. How did we end up here?" He glanced at the others, who all shrugged.

"They somehow figured out how to mind control Fae despite our mind blocks. This is extremely concerning."

"How many of the guards here are actually working for the Council of their own free will?" Grey asked.

"I don't know," Fenrick peered around at the townspeople. "But we need to get out of here before they call more guards."

"You have a choice to make," I said to the guards. "We're leaving here, now. Are you with us or the Council?"

"I want to take those snakes down," the same man said.

"Then we need a way out of here without the Fae here following us. Do you know a place that's safe?" I asked.

"We don't know what's safe anymore, Princess. I can't remember what atrocities we committed when we were under their control. I'm sorry, I failed my kingdom." He hung his head.

"Not your fault, but we really need to get out of here." I glanced around the village.

"I think I know a place." Grey frowned. "If it's still there and warded after all these years."

"Are you helping us or the Council?" I asked the ten men around us. "You need to decide now. We aren't taking anyone with us who is assisting the Council."

The men all dropped to their knees again and bowed to me.

"I swear fealty to the Princess of the Shadow Court. I swear my sword and my protection to any monarch to come after Princess Aurelia and her Shifter King," the first man said, and the others followed along.

I was stunned but breathed out a sigh. They were actually on our side. Things were looking up if we had more trained soldiers with us.

Was it possible that there were others in Faery who were also under the Council's control? Could I lift the mind control on all of them to build our army?

"Please rise. We need to run, because the locals are getting restless." I peered around at the villagers.

They didn't want to hurt us, I was sure, but their survival was more important than their morals. The Council had the realm right where they wanted them. They would do anything to survive, and I had a feeling that was exactly why Ronaldo had started taxing them.

It was disgusting, and I had every intention of destroying him for it. He'd already earned his death by my hand a hundred times over, but this was going too far.

"Let's go." Grey wrapped a hand around my wrist and pulled me away from the soldiers.

"Wait." I turned back to the Shadow Guards. "Can you sift us out? Somewhere in the forest where the townspeople won't be able to follow?"

"Yes, Your Highness," the same man said, bowing his head.

He held out a hand to me, but Grey was there first. "You take us together, and do not touch my mate."

I stared up at Grey with wide eyes. He was always possessive, but why was he acting like that with new allies? The guard had sworn fealty to me. He wasn't going to hurt me. I needed to have a talk with him and the others about the overprotective bullshit they were constantly pulling.

It was getting stifling, especially when we all knew I was the key to stopping the Council.

The man simply nodded and took Grey's hand. He'd sworn fealty to Grey and any future monarchs as well. That was good enough for me.

Apparently, Grey wasn't as convinced. He pulled me into his arms, and we were sucked into a swirl of time and space.

I had to trust we would be safe even though I had no idea where the hell we were going.

Chapter 8

GREY

THE WORLD SPUN around us and dropped us into the middle of the forest. It was a dark and gloomy place, and I recognized it instantly.

"This isn't the same forest we were just in," I said, pulling my sword from its sheath. "Why did you bring us here?"

"You said you might know of somewhere to hide out," the man said. "I brought you to the dark forest."

"What's your name?" I asked.

"Talon, your majesty." He bowed his head, and I flinched.

I wasn't the Shifter King yet. I was no one's majesty and wouldn't be even after this was all over. It wasn't who I was. I may have been the rightful Shifter King, but that didn't mean I wanted everyone bowing and scraping at my feet.

"Talon, I'm Grey, and you will call me that. I do recognize the dark forest. It was just outside my home, but where are the others?" I peered around the blackened, gnarled trees, but none of the others had sifted in yet.

I didn't like this. I pulled Aurelia behind me, still not trusting the Fae, even after his oath. It hadn't been made in blood, and I never trusted an oath not sealed with blood. We couldn't exactly spill blood in the village for an oath when we were running from the Council, though.

"The others are right behind us, I'm sure," Talon said.

I narrowed my eyes at him. "How can you be sure?"

"We have a mind link. The king made sure his men could communicate in battle, but when we were controlled by the Council, I'm not sure if it worked or not. I'm hoping they got my message."

"So we're waiting here, hoping that the others got your message?" I threw my hands up in frustration.

Aurelia placed a calming hand on my back, and I took a cleansing breath. I still didn't like this, but at least we were close to shifter territory and a place I could protect my mate. I hoped.

"We are. They will be here soon, I'm sure of it." Talon scanned the forest with a hopeful expression.

I crossed my arms over my chest as I waited.

This had better not be a trap. I will not hesitate to shift and rip the Fae apart with my teeth.

I bared my teeth at the man as Aurelia stepped around me.

"They will be here, Grey. I know he's not lying to us." Aurelia rested her hand on my biceps.

"How can you possibly know that, Aurelia?" I asked. "You trust too easily. I love that about you, but it also scares the hell out of me."

I closed my eyes and tilted my head back. I needed to protect her, but how could I do that when she was constantly getting into situations just like this? She was too trusting. Talon watched us warily as another guard popped into existence.

My shoulders tensed, and I reached for my sword before I realized the guard had Asher with him.

"Where are the others?" I asked Ash as I took a step closer to him.

Ash smirked. "Worried about us? They are being transported, but as soon as you and the princess left, the villagers went a little feral and tried to attack."

"What?" Aurelia shrieked.

I pulled her in to my side to comfort her. "They are all warriors, mate. They will be fine."

"How can you possibly know that?" She clenched her fists in the fabric of my shirt. "There were so many people there, they would have been horribly outnumbered."

Ash shook his head. "The people in that village were not trained in combat. They didn't stand a chance against trained warriors, Princess. Your father and Fenrick are fine."

"Then where are they? Why aren't they here with you?" she shrieked.

I pulled her against me with my hand on the back of her head in reassurance. "They will be fine, my love, and if they aren't here in the next five minutes, we'll go back for them. I promise."

She blinked back her tears as she stared up at me. "They better be here in five minutes unharmed, or the Council is going to have a battle on their hands much sooner than they ever expected."

"There's my bloodthirsty mate." I chuckled and kissed her forehead.

I would make sure that the Council paid if anything happened to the king or Fenrick. These people had become important to me simply because they were important to Aurelia. It was a new feeling. One I hadn't felt in more than two centuries. This princess was like a bulldozer when she came into my life and changed every fucking thing.

"I'm not bloodthirsty," she growled.

Ash cleared his throat. "I want to go back and help them."

"No need." Fenrick's voice sounded behind me.

I spun with Aurelia still tucked into my chest to find Fenrick, the Shadow King and the rest of the mind-controlled guards standing behind me.

"Thank Fates," I sighed. "We need to find shelter."

"I thought you knew of a place," Fenrick said with a raised brow.

"I do, but we were waiting for you. Took you long enough."

"Those people were crazy. I get that they're starving, but they were like animals, and we didn't want to hurt them." Fenrick turned his gaze on my mate.

She was the reason they had shied away from hurting the villagers. She wouldn't have liked it. We were in the midst of a war, and she was too kindhearted for death and destruction. She was the same way with the Secret Service agents.

How were we going to defeat the Council when she refused to use her magic to hurt others unless they absolutely deserved it? That was why we continued to protect her. We couldn't afford for her hesitation when it came down to her life or someone else's.

I would burn the realms to the ground if they hurt her because she wavered.. I would not hesitate to destroy everything. She was my everything. As I stared at Ash, the king, and Fenrick, I realized they would do the same.

I sniffed the air and peered around the forest to get my bearings. My sense of direction wasn't as great as it once was, but I leaned into Aurelia. "Can you ask the trees where we are?"

Aurelia nodded and pulled away from my arms to set her hand on the nearest trunk. She flinched slightly as she spoke to the tree.

"We are about a mile west of the Shifter King's castle." She stared at me.

"Good. We should be able to get to the safe house pretty quickly then." I nodded and headed toward the castle.

My own personal hideout as a pup wasn't far away. I'd had wards set up and I hoped that those wards were still there, and the Council hadn't taken over my personal space. I'd had a witch that was extremely powerful set them.

Could Aurelia get through them too? I guessed she could because the wards at the Syndicate were strong, and she could get past them just fine. It would help my mate to be able to get through them in a time of crisis, especially if she needed to sift there.

"Where is this place?" Aurelia asked.

"Shifter territory," I said as I wrapped my hand around hers.

We raced through the woods like the Riders of the Hunt were on our ass, but of course they weren't because Asher was with us. We burst through the tree line to the perimeter of the house I'd left behind more than two centuries ago.

Everything looked exactly the same. I raised a hand to the wards, and they buzzed briefly beneath my palm. They were still there, which meant that no one had crossed without my knowledge. Well, at least no one who wasn't stronger than the witch who'd cast them.

"It doesn't appear to be tampered with, but I'd still like to do a perimeter sweep before we assume it's safe," I said.

"Agreed," Aurelia said with a nod.

"You're not sweeping the perimeter. You're staying with your father and Fenrick, where it's safe." I glared down at her.

"Oh, I'm not? And who made that decision?" Aurelia asked, crossing her arms over her chest.

"I did. I'm your mate and I can't even begin to explain what the fuck I would do if something happened to you. You are mine, and I will not back down where your safety is concerned."

"You all have got to be kidding me." She threw her hands up in the air.

Her father and Fenrick had taken up positions on either side of her as I spoke the words that would probably damn me with her for eternity. I refused to let her become a casualty. The place was warded, but I wouldn't take chances with her life. She was the key to everything.

If the Council had gotten inside the protection to ambush us and I didn't check first and lost her, we were all doomed. The others more than me, because I would become the monster the Council thought I was. I would become the threat.

She glanced between Fenrick and her father, who both peered at her with pleading eyes and sighed. "Fine. I'll stay here, but you can't protect me from this war. I'm the key to everything and I will have to fight."

I ignored the wolf in my head that growled angrily, not wanting our mate anywhere near the impending that. All he knew was his mate was in danger. Is that why I was lashing out now? He was being a pain in the ass and pushing me to hide her from everyone.

Instead, I ran the perimeter in wolf form and searched for anything that could possibly harm us while there but there was nothing. Could it have really been fully warded for all these years?

When I got back to Aurelia, I shook my onyx head. My mate dug her fingers into my fur, rubbing between my ears. I shifted quickly, much to my wolf's protests.

"I didn't find anything problematic." I shook my head. "The wards have held. I think we could make this our hideout."

"We aren't hiding from the Council. We are biding our time until we can take them down." Aurelia shoved at my chest.

"I know that, my love, but we need to lay low for a while until we can figure out what to do." I scanned the clearing.

"You don't need to treat me like a liability, though." She crossed her arms over her chest and marched past the wards.

She was walking away from all of us. I glanced at the others, and they shrugged. What the hell was going wrong? She wasn't being reasonable. She didn't even know the house she was walking into was safe.

"You're not a liability, you're my life!" I shouted at her back.

"Then maybe you should remember that I'm not a baby or a helpless female!" she called back.

"You're neither of those things," I said as I stomped to the house.

If she was going to be angry and walk away, I was going to follow her and make her realize what was really going on. I would do anything for her. Anything to keep her safe, no matter the consequences for the world.

She was mine, and I didn't care how mad she got about my need to protect her. I would do it a thousand times over, and she couldn't stop me.

"Aurelia, stop. I haven't checked the house!" I yelled.

"No!" she yelled back. "I don't answer to you or anyone."

"We don't know if it's safe," I growled.

"I don't care, I'm strong. I can take care of myself, and I need to crash, so leave me alone." She turned to me with a glare.

Shit. Had I crossed too many lines with my mate? Was she done with me? I moved faster to her, ready to pull her into my arms, but was she right? Was I being an ass?

We couldn't defeat the Council if we were fighting among ourselves. I needed to get my mate to see there wasn't a problem. She needed to realize that I was on her side, no matter what.

Chapter 9

AURELIA

I STORMED into the beautiful old house fuming. Why did he act like that? What made him think I wasn't capable of taking care of myself?

The anger bubbled up as I pushed through the double doors and stepped inside. Dust puffed up in my face and I coughed. Yes, it was old and had been sitting unused for centuries, but the amount of dust was slightly alarming.

I waved a hand in front of my face and stepped further inside. It would be beautiful if it were cleaned up. There were worn sofas under vaulted ceilings, but there were no decorations of any kind.

"Aurelia, where are you going?" Grey shouted behind me.

I stomped through the house and down the hallway. I didn't want to be in the same room with the overbearing asshole right then.

"I'm going to find somewhere to sleep. *Alone*!" I yelled back.

Maybe I was being dramatic, but I was tired of everyone thinking I was helpless. I was the one who'd stopped the mind control on the guards outside, not any of them.

"We don't know if it's safe," Grey called again.

"And I'm the most powerful person in the room, so I will be fine." I waved a hand over my shoulder.

At the end of the hall there was a door that I shoved open. A huge bed sat against the back wall and a bedside table was on each side. It was perfect for a nap. I crept inside, but the heat at my back let me know I wasn't alone.

An angry shifter was right behind me. Great. He couldn't just give me a little time to myself? I spun on him and poked a finger into his chest. "I said I wanted to be alone."

"And my father always taught me to never go to bed angry with your mate, so we're going to have this argument now." Grey crossed his arms over his chest and crowded closer.

His woodsy scent filled my nose as I sucked in a breath. That wasn't going to help me stay mad at him. My shoulders slumped.

"What do you want, Grey? I'm tired." I shook my head.

"We need to check that it's safe before you sleep," he said.

He reached for me, but I backed away. I was tired of proving myself and demonstrating I was different from everyone else, only to be coddled and treated like a child.

"Then check the house already. I need rest. Do you have any idea how exhausting that magic was?" I shoved at his chest.

It was the wrong move. I knew it the second I touched his sculpted pecs. He pushed forward and crowded me until my hands were pinned between us.

"Do you have any idea what I would do to the world if something happened to you?" He cupped my cheek.

I turned my face away so I couldn't see the fire in his eyes and did my best not to breathe through my nose as I glared at the floor.

"You are treating me like a helpless damsel in distress when we both know that I'm anything but. I saved you from the Council prison." My gaze clashed with his.

"I would be the monster the Council expects me to be if anything happened to you, Aurelia. I would burn the world and anyone who ever hurt you or looked at you wrong. Know that. You. Are. Mine. Mine to love and mine to fucking protect."

I gasped at his words and the glowing intensity of his eyes. He was serious. He would destroy the world for me.

"Don't do that. I need you to see me as an equal. You and the others are constantly surrounding me in a fight, guarding me like I'm some kind of porcelain doll that needs protecting or I might shatter. How do I prove more than I already have that I'm not going to break?" I threw my hands up in the air.

"I do see you as an equal. Hell, you're better than me in every way. You are the one who made it possible to go home. You are everything to me, and the idea of losing you makes me crazy," Grey growled.

He slammed his lips against mine in a brutal kiss. I tried to push his chest, but my fingers gripped the shirt he was wearing and pulled him closer instead.

He was mine as I was his. I just wished he gave me the same consideration I was giving him. I didn't coddle him the way he did me, but all thoughts tumbled out of my head as he wrapped his arms around me and plastered his chest to mine.

"I love you, mate. I will do anything for you. I will try to be better," he said between heated kisses.

"I love you too, but sometimes the overbearing alpha bullshit pisses me off." I glared at him.

Grey gripped my ass, pulling me impossibly closer. "Then how about we fuck all that anger out before our nap... together."

"I told you I was taking a nap alone."

"Then I guess I have to grovel a bit to get you to let me sleep with you again." His sexy grin held all kinds of dirty promises.

"How do you plan on doing that?" I shoved him back successfully this time.

"You'll see." He grinned.

He crowded me until I was backed against the wall. "What are you doing?"

"Showing you how I'm going to grovel." He pressed his lips to the hollow at my neck.

I shuddered under his touch. I could never deny him, even angry. He was mine. His lips trailed down my neck and his tongue poked out to lick at the spot where he would mark me for real one day. I squirmed but couldn't move because I was pinned against the wall.

"Grey," I moaned.

He gripped my ass and pulled me even closer until the hard outline of his cock rubbed against my belly.

"What do you want mate?" he asked, his hot breath fanning over my neck.

"I want you," I groaned. "But I also want you to see me for who I really am and not someone who needs to be kept in a tower."

"I know that's not you, Aurelia. I love every part of you, even the stubborn parts." He chuckled against my skin as his lips traveled lower.

He squeezed my ass again and rubbed his cock over my thigh.

"Then prove it," I challenged.

"Gladly." He grinned and lifted me off the ground.

I wrapped my legs around his waist as he moved me over to the bed. He laid me down on the dusty comforter and pulled my shirt off over my head and stared down at my heaving chest. My skin prickled with heat everywhere his gaze touched.

He kissed down my body and his fingers trailed over my shoulders, pushing down the straps of my bra. I shivered under his attention. Reaching back, I unclasped my bra and let it fall to the bed. Grey groaned and pinched one nipple between his fingers. He swirled his tongue around the other, and my back arched into him, giving him better access.

His fingers trailed down my body to my core and he pushed his hand beneath the pants I was wearing, never even bothering to take them off before he circled my clit with his thumb. I gripped his shoulders as I squirmed beneath him.

"I love the way you grip me like I'm everything in the world to you, mate," Grey growled against my breasts.

My nails dug into his skin even harder at the added vibrations. I was going to come while half-dressed just from this. How did he do this to me? How did he make me feel both treasured and desired at the same time?

"Grey," I moaned. "What are you doing to me?"

"I'm about to make you scream." He glanced up at me with a devilish smile before pulling his hand from my pants and popping the button.

I whimpered at the loss of him where I needed him most, but the bastard just chuckled. He sat back on his knees, his eyes hooded as he stared down at my heaving body. I wiggled my hips to get him to do something, but he just continued to peer down at me.

It would have been unnerving if he'd been anyone but Grey. I ran my hands over my breasts and down my belly. If he was just going to stare, I would give him a show. A strangled moan escaped him as I shoved my hand inside my pants and circled my clit with fumbling fingers.

Grey's eyes glowed with his wolf, and he flew into action. He gripped the waistband of my jeans and pulled them down. His gaze zeroed in on where I was touching myself, and he gripped my inner thighs, pushing them wide for a better view.

"You're wearing too many clothes," I said, breathless.

Grey jumped off the bed and flung his shirt over his head before ripping his jeans off in seconds. All his tanned, toned skin was on display just for me. My gaze roamed over him as he stalked back to the bed. His hand pumped his cock slowly as he watched me. My back arched as tingles raced down my spine.

"Grey, fuck. I need you."

I wasn't about to give myself an orgasm when I had him right there. He smirked and kneeled on the bed.

"What do you need, mate?" he asked.

"I need you to fuck me." I gripped his shoulders in an effort to pull him down on me, but he was too strong.

I huffed in annoyance when he resisted, but the next second, he gripped my thighs and pulled closer. His cock lined up with my entrance, but he didn't push inside. He rubbed his cock up my slit and over my clit. Stars burst behind my eyes as he continued his game, and my head thrashed.

"You're so fucking responsive, my love." He finally pushed inside, and the intrusion was just what I needed.

My walls gripped his length, and he growled as he pulled out and slammed back in, hitting that spot that had a rainbow of colors dancing behind my eyes. I screamed as white-hot euphoria blasted through every inch of my body. My ears rang and I barely heard his curses over the white noise in my mind. I was floating.

With a final roar, Grey thrust into me harder and faster, hitting that spot again and again before emptying himself inside me and collapsing on top of me.

We were both breathing heavily as he rolled to the side and pulled me into his chest. His hands rubbed soothing circles on my back as he kissed my forehead.

"It's not in my nature to let my mate jump headfirst into danger, my love." He rested his chin on the top of my head. "But I'll try to stop being so overbearing and protective."

"We aren't going to have a choice soon, Grey. The Council is coming for me, and I'm the only one who can stop them."

Why would the Fates rest this all firmly on my shoulders alone? It seemed like an impossible task, but one I had to face, no matter the consequences.

Chapter 10
GREY

"**THE HOUSE IS SECURE,**" Fenrick said as we walked out of the bedroom. "Though there is two centuries worth of dust caked everywhere."

"That's to be expected." I shrugged.

"I still think we should look for more Council guards that have been controlled by the Council," Aurelia said, crossing her arms.

"I don't want you going after the Council's guards just to see if you can do to them what you did with your father's men. It feels like a risk." My wolf growled in my head in agreement.

He was riding me hard to keep our mate protected, but after the conversation I'd just had with her, I knew that wasn't practical. She was part of this whether I liked it or not. My wolf was just going to have to learn to get over the fact that his mate was stronger than him and be done with it.

"I'm not going in without a plan, or setting myself up as bait, Grey. If you would just listen." She glared at me.

Shit. I was fucking everything up. "Sorry, my wolf is being a pain in my ass."

"It's fine." She sighed. "I think the guards should go back to their posts and pretend they are still on the Council's side. They can send word when they discover a new group of blank-eyed guards so I can try to heal their minds."

Ash stepped forward, grinning. "That's a good tactical plan that puts you in as little danger as possible, Princess. I like it."

He wasn't wrong. The plan was solid, and while the guards were out searching for others, we could still track down the rebels.

Fenrick nodded. "It makes sense. We could divide and conquer, with both groups looking for something different. If we succeed in both, we might actually stand a chance against the Council."

"Agreed," I said, and Aurelia's gaze snapped to mine.

"You're agreeing? Even though we have no idea if I will be able to clear the others of mind control?" Her gaze flicked back and forth between my eyes, searching for something.

"My love, we all know you'll be able to do it again. You're the only one unsure. We all believe in you." I wrapped my arms around her.

"Then why fight it?" she asked.

"I thought you were planning to take unnecessary risks. You have a track record of doing that in the past."

"Only to save you, you big, dumb wolf." She laid her head on my chest and my heart thumped harder.

It scared the hell out of me and made me proud at the same time that she would risk herself for me. I leaned down and kissed the top of her head again.

"No more risking yourself, especially not for me," I whispered into her hair.

"I make no promises on that, wolf." Her words were muffled in my chest, but I still heard them.

How could I make this woman see that there was no life for me without her in it? There was no life for anyone without her... well, none that anyone wanted. If the Council won the upcoming battles, they would enslave everyone. We had to stop them before their greed won out and doomed us all.

"Let's get back to the plan," Ash said, clapping me on the back.

He was right. This wasn't a conversation for mixed company. The guards peered at us with amusement, like watching their princess spar with the Shifter King was the highlight of their day. It probably was, since they couldn't remember most of it because of the mind control.

Aurelia turned to the guards and straightened, rolling her shoulders back as she peered at every man in turn. "Do you think you can do this? Can you pretend to be under their control? What about the villagers who saw you run off with us?"

The leader of the group stepped forward and bowed his head to us both in turn before he spoke. "It would be our pleasure to deceive the Council and save our fellow warriors from their mind control. We will gladly accept this task."

"What about the villagers?" Aurelia chewed her bottom lip.

"We will tell them that we followed you to apprehend you, but you escaped us." He clasped his hands in front of him.

"It's a smart plan." Fenrick nodded.

"Okay, but if the Council finds out, I want you to get out of there immediately. I won't risk people. I can't." Aurelia wrung her hands together.

"On your order, Princess. If we are found out, we will abort the mission." He bowed again and placed a fist over his heart.

The men filed out and I wrapped my arms around my mate once more. "You're going to be the best queen."

"Someday, but only if we can conquer the Council. The only way to beat them is to find the rebels. Easier said than done." She sighed.

There's a town a little larger than the village we were in on the other side of the dark forest. We should check there," Fenrick said.

"Hopefully, there's no one who can see through glamour there." I rubbed my eyes.

"We'll need different disguises this time, since the Council will probably be looking for those." Aurelia huffed.

She stepped away from me and closed her eyes. She was so beautiful she took my breath away at times. I still couldn't believe she was mine. That she forgave me for the mess with Dan and her foster mother. It was a miracle we were all here.

Her body transformed before my eyes, and I grinned at the black-haired beauty standing in front of me.

Fenrick gripped my shoulder, and cool magic washed over me in a wave as the glamour slid into place. I was just lucky shifters weren't allowed back in Faery yet, because they would sniff me out a mile away.

"We all good?" I asked, my voice a rasp.

It still amazed me how far Fae glamour could go. It changed me into a different person entirely.

"We are good to go," Fenrick confirmed.

He gripped both mine and Aurelia's arms while the Shadow King held out a hand to Ash. We were swirling in time and space in a matter of seconds.

My feet hit the soft, packed dirt a second later, and I caught Aurelia before she stumbled and fell. The chattering of Fae met my ears from the other side of the tree line. Fenrick had sifted us to the other side of the dark forest.

"They've already heard that the king is back somewhere in Faery. But the excitement doesn't appear to be because they think they're going to be saved. Several are openly discussing the reward. We need to be wary." I clenched my fists at my sides.

"We'll be careful," Aurelia promised and patted my arm.

"I know you will be." I held my hand out to her, and she placed her hand in mine. "Because you're not leaving my side."

Aurelia rolled her now green eyes but didn't comment further. I was grateful for that, because that meant she would listen to me just this once.

"Let's try the local pub. We can have a meal and get some information." Fenrick strode to the village.

We followed along behind him, and I kept my hand in Aurelia's the whole way. We walked past Fae, but all chatter died away as they saw us striding through their little town.

Were they wary of strangers? Several older Fae glared in my direction and some just scurried into their homes, slamming the door shut behind them.

"I'm not getting a welcoming vibe here," I whispered.

"They're scared," Aurelia said. "The Council is taking everything from them, and newcomers must be suspected now."

"The Council has spies everywhere," Fenrick agreed. "Any strange people in town are suspicious. I get it, but it's going to make this twice as hard."

The Shadow King squeezed Fenrick's shoulder. "That's why we're going to the pub. People get drunk and let things slip out in mixed company."

Fenrick's plan was solid, but as we rounded the corner to the pub, whispers floated to me. The word rebellion caught my attention and I flinched, stopping in my tracks.

"You all go ahead. I'm going to check something out, real quick." I squeezed Aurelia's hand before I let go.

"I thought we were sticking together," she said.

"It's probably nothing, but I overheard a whispered conversation. I just want to check it out. I'll be inside in a few minutes." I strode away from the group and rounded the corner of the pub.

Two men stood at the back of the stone building with their heads together, whispering about something I couldn't quite make out.

"You're part of the rebellion," I whispered so only they could hear me.

Both men flinched and spun on me, magic flaring in their hands. "There is no rebellion. What kind of nonsense are you speaking?"

"I was told by a powerful seer to seek out the rebellion. That's you, right?" I was still whispering so I didn't bring unwanted attention to the conversation, but the men before me had no such issues.

"The powerful seer was wrong, or maybe you're a spy for the Council," the same man spoke, crossing his arms over his chest, his bushy eyebrows pinched down in a scowl.

"I'm the last thing from a Council spy." I laughed.

I couldn't help it, that was the farthest thing from the truth.

The other man took a threatening step forward. "If you're not a spy, then you're working against them and there's a hefty reward out for any Council dissenters."

"Give us one good reason why we shouldn't call the guards and have you arrested for questioning," bushy eyebrow guy said.

"Because we both know it won't just be for questioning. The Council is on a massive power trip." I planted my hands on my hips.

"Plus, I could take you both down before you even opened your mouth to call for the guards."

The men glanced at each other warily and then back to me. I held my hands up in the air.

"I don't want to do that. We're on the same side, I think, but I won't be taken by the Council again, so take your pick." I clenched and unclenched my fists at my side.

My wolf was snarling in my head. He wanted out and to prove who the Shifter King really was. I couldn't shift though, since it would blow my cover.

"What do you want?" the bushy eyebrow guy asked.

Magic filled his palms again. He didn't believe me and was ready for a fight. I didn't blame him. His life was on the line if he was found out by the Council.

"I just want to talk. I need to find the rebellion."

"I already told you the rebellion doesn't exist. We've all been thoroughly beaten into submission by the Council. We couldn't rebel if we tried. Take that back to the Council," bushy eyebrow guy snarled.

The other guy stepped forward, who also had magic pooling in his hands. They were ready for a fight, and clearly convinced I was working with the Council.

How bad would it be if I shifted in that back alley and showed them once and for all that I definitely wasn't working for the Council?

No. If I shifted, they would know who I was and I couldn't let that happen until I knew for sure they were rebels.

I guess I have a fight on my hands. I hope this doesn't destroy any chance we have of the rebels aiding us in the war.

Chapter 11
AURELIA

"WHERE IS HE?" I asked, chewing my lip nervously.

He was taking too long, and it was making me twitchy. Was Grey okay? Maybe I should have gone with him.

"He'll be fine, daughter." My father patted my shoulder.

He couldn't know that for sure though. We had no idea what Grey was facing behind the pub. What if the men he confronted had called the guards and I wasn't there to clear them from the mind control? What if he was attacked? Could he stop his wolf from shifting?

I shifted uncomfortably in my seat as a woman brought over five bowls of some kind of stew and drinks for us all, but Grey still wasn't back yet.

"I need to go check on him," I grumbled.

"You're not going anywhere alone." Ash gripped my arm lightly. "He'll have my ass if I let you go out there."

"You all are a bunch of cavemen." I threw my hands up.

Why couldn't any of them stop this?

"She's right," Fenrick said with a sigh. "He's been gone too long. I think we need to check."

"See?" I glared at Ash and my father. "Fenrick and I will go check, and you two stay here."

"No, we aren't splitting up again. We all go or none of us." Ash crossed his arms over his chest.

"Fine, but what about the food?" I asked. "We still need to eat."

"We'll come back as soon as we find Grey," my father said and waved a hand to the woman behind the bar.

He handed her some coins and her eyes widened in surprise. "Give those bowls to anyone in need we will be back to eat after we find my daughter's mate."

The woman nodded and dropped the coins in her pocket before hurrying to clear the bowls from the table and shuffled to the back.

"That was nice," I said, grinning at my father.

"I hate seeing what the Council has done to my people," he growled under his breath.

"We'll fix this." I stormed out the door, the men grumbling behind me.

I rounded the same corner that Grey had and gasped at the scene in front of me. Two men were standing in front of Grey, their glittering magic pooled in their palms.

"What's going on here?" I asked as I stepped closer.

Grey's shoulders bunched up at the tone of my voice and he glanced at me over his shoulder. "Go back inside, love. I have this under control."

"No, I'm not going back inside. They are threatening you." I took a step toward the men.

My shadows appeared on my arms, writhing with anger. Their eyes widened in horror as they stepped back.

"You're a Shadow Fae?" the one to the left with really big eyebrows whispered.

"I am." I grinned. "Now, do you want to tell me what is going on here?"

"You're in league with him. We'll tell the Council that you're dissenters and we will be rewarded," he said loudly.

My father gripped my arm and pulled me back. I glanced over my shoulder to see his head cocked to the side. "Teo, is that you?"

"How do you know that name?" the man asked.

"Bram! Shit. What are two of my best guards doing in this little town?" My father dropped his glamour for a second and both men cursed.

"You know them?" I asked, frowning at my father. "You could have led with that, Dad."

"We can't talk here." Teo scanned the empty alley. "How did you get here? Where have you been?"

"Not here," I said. "You already said it's not safe."

"We're looking for the rebellion," Father whispered.

Bram and Teo glanced at each other and then glared at Grey.

"You vouch for him?" Bram sneered.

I edged closer to Grey, my shadows still swirling along my arms, begging for a reason to put them in their places. My father pushed me gently toward Grey and stepped in front of me.

"Of course, I vouch for him. He's my daughter's mate and the Shifter King." He raised a brow at the men, who both cursed and glanced at Grey with wide eyes.

"You're the princess? Shit," Bram said softly.

"We need get you out of here. The town is crawling with Council guards." Teo waved for us to follow him further down the alley.

"Dad, are you sure about them? They threatened to take us to the Council," I whispered.

"Yes, daughter. They are two of my most loyal warriors."

"Okay," I said and followed the two Fae.

I hoped I wasn't following them to the destruction of the realms, because that was what it felt like. I gripped Grey's hand in mine as Asher and Fenrick closed in on us from both sides. When did the loyalties shift?

Fenrick was next to Grey and Ash was at my elbow. I glanced up at him warily, but he just winked at me.

"I take my promises seriously, Princess. I will protect you until the end of this war and until you stop requiring my protection."

"My magic could put you on your ass, you know." I raised a brow, but a gust of wind hit me, and onyx hair flew into my face.

Ash chuckled and called his magic back. I stuck my tongue out at him and directed the shadows to shove him back. He stumbled but righted himself quickly.

"You play dirty. I like it."

"Don't ever forget it," I said.

Teo and Bram stopped in front of a decrepit building, the door barely hanging on by a single hinge. I shot them a dubious look because this wasn't what I'd expected for the underground hideout for the resistance.

"Are you sure this is where we want to go?" I asked. "It feels like a trap."

"It's not a trap, I swear it," Teo said. "It's just a safe place to talk."

I glanced at my father dubiously for confirmation, and he nodded. It was now or never. If we wasted this opportunity, we may never find it again. Grey squeezed my hip in reassurance, and I followed the strange men into the gloom.

Bram lit a small oil lamp once we were all inside and away from the door. Teo walked around the room, his hands pointing to the walls as they glowed a soft yellow. Was he putting up wards? I needed to learn how to do that if Fae were able to.

"It's safe to speak now," Teo said as he took a seat next to Bram.

Bram waved a hand for us to sit around the wooden table and get comfortable. "This conversation may take a while, so you might as well sit."

We took the offered seats, and I was sandwiched in between Ash and Grey. They were cavemen who always had to protect me, but I got it... sometimes.

"How did you get out of the castle?" my father asked. "Everyone was either sent to cells or mind controlled if they didn't cave willingly to the Council's demands."

"Can you drop your glamour? It's weird talking to strangers when so many of them have been Council plants lately." Teo frowned.

I dropped my glamour, and both men bowed, cursing themselves for the way they'd behaved before.

"Princess, please forgive us. We didn't know who you were." Bram practically laid his head on the table in front of him.

"I was glamoured. It's fine. Please rise." I glanced around, shifting uncomfortably in my seat. "Tell us how you escaped the Council."

"We weren't at the palace when everything went down. We were here visiting with family," Bram said.

"A few days after the Council ransacked the castle, word got to us here that the king was in prison and the Council now ruled. We were set to head back to the castle but hid in these tunnels until it was safe to return and search for survivors." Teo shook his head.

"We found a couple men huddled in the passageways practically starved and brought them back here."

I gasped at those words. I had been in the castle and had only ever encountered one person. Had I not searched hard enough? I hung my head as tears burned the back of my eyes. I could have helped them, but I didn't look hard enough for survivors.

Grey pulled me to his side and rubbed my back. I buried my face in his neck to stop anyone from seeing my weakness.

"Princess, what is it?" Teo asked, leaning over the table.

"I could have saved them." I sniffled.

"What? No. They were well trained to hide in the tunnels if the Council ever came. You weren't at the castle. There's nothing you could have done." Teo shook his head.

"I was at the castle. I searched for survivors in the dungeons and only found one Fae that wasn't hostile." I sniffed again. "I should have searched harder."

Bram straightened and stared me down. "Those men are alive, Princess. They went through hell, but they are alive. You did not fail them by not finding them, and they are on our side."

It helped a little to know they were alive, but they'd still suffered because I hadn't been strong enough to fight the Council then. How many people had suffered because I was too weak to stand up to Ronaldo and his fucking Council?

"We need to find the rebels. We need an army. I'm working on parts of the army, but we just aren't sure we'll have enough men to take them down." I ran a hand down my face.

"The rebels want the monarchy back. They just don't think it's possible with the king in prison or possibly dead. The Council has spread many rumors." Bram clenched his hand into a fist.

"The king is right here," my father said. "And I'm disgusted with the taxes and the slavery the Council is subjecting the people to. We had to flee the closest village to the castle because they are basically slaves, and the Council isn't giving them enough to survive on. It's horrific."

"Most of the people there tend the fields," Teo said.

"Yes, and they still are but they are only given enough rations for one person even though many have families to feed. They are starving and desperate. They need help, and the only way we can do that is to take down the Council, and the only way we can do that is with the help of the rebels." My father slammed his fist on the table.

"We'll take you to the rebels as soon as we can, but I just want us all to get on the same page first." Bram leaned back in his chair.

"It seems like we're all on the same page already." I crossed my arms over my chest.

"How did you get out of prison?" Teo asked my father.

"Aurelia busted us all out." He nodded to me with a hint of pride.

"Zeke helped a lot," I mumbled and glanced at Ash.

I hoped that I didn't bring up a bunch of bad shit for him. The night when Zeke was shot blasted through my memories without my consent, and my shoulders slumped. The loss was still too fresh. It had only been days since we'd left Zeke bleeding on the ground.

My father took over the conversation, obviously realizing that I needed a minute to compose myself. "They got us out of the prison even if it was in an unconventional way."

"I may have blown a few hundred gallons of their mind control serum sky high." I shrugged.

Zeke was still on my mind, and Ash seemed to realize it. He placed his hand on my shoulder and squeezed it gently.

"I think we're all caught up. Now, can you please take us to the rebels? We don't have time to spare." I grimaced as I stood.

"Yes, Princess. We can take you to the rebels now," Teo said, and I smiled.

Hopefully, the rebels would help our cause because if they didn't, I had no idea what else we would do.

Chapter 12

GREY

"OKAY," Bram said as he pushed up from the table. "Let's go to the rebellion."

Instead of taking us back the way he came, he moved through the room to a different door that was shrouded in shadows.

Where were they taking us? I wrapped an arm around Aurelia's waist and followed the men as they opened another door. It was dank and cold as they led us down the corridor. What the fuck was happening? Why was I following these Fae into the dark tunnels without any real assurance that we would be safe?

The king trusted them, but was that enough? The king had blindly followed the Council for centuries. Was this more of the same?

I pushed Aurelia behind me and nodded to Ash and Fenrick. The two of them didn't need any more encouragement than that to close ranks at her sides. Aurelia huffed, and I glanced back just in time to see her roll her eyes.

"Don't argue," I said under my breath.

"I have no intention of arguing," she said with a grin.

"Good." I nodded to Fenrick and Ash to stay close and continued to follow the two men who'd accosted me in the alley.

They had been assholes, and I still didn't trust anywhere they planned to take us. No matter what the king said, I would have my guard up when it came to Aurelia's safety. Her safety always came first, and the king knew that as well as I did.

We traveled through the tunnels to who knew where and the longer we traveled, the more wary I was. It could have been an elaborate trap set by the Council and the guards Aurelia had freed with her magic. Were they really in on it with the Council and seeing exactly what my mate would go through to help her people?

"Here we are!" Bram yelled and threw his arms out wide. "Welcome to the resistance."

Did he have to play up the dramatics? The entire room went silent. The sounds of swords clashing subsided as everyone turned to stare at us.

There were people of all walks of life in the huge space into which we strolled. I even noticed some Shadow Fae with shadows writhing over their arms. They were trying to learn from the centuries-old Fae how to wield them, even though my mate had all but mastered them in a few short months.

A man on a dais stood as he saw us walk through the passageway, glaring at our group. I didn't like the look he was giving us. We're we going to be handed over to the Council?

We didn't have our glamours on, so the whispers from the group on the ground all spoke of the kings and the princess. Some even recognized Fenrick as Aurelia's guardian.

They knew who we were, so why weren't they welcoming us? We were obviously on the same side.

"Santori," the king boomed, taking a step toward the man on the dais. "Is that you?"

"My king? It can't be." The man took a step toward us. "How did you escape the Council?"

The king turned to Aurelia and nodded with pride. "My daughter saved us all. She's going to save the realms as well."

"That's little Aurelia?" The man cocked his head to the side as he rushed to us from his spot on the dais. "You're so big."

"I'm an adult now, yes." Aurelia said, crossing her arms.

"Yes, I apologize. I meant you've grown up. The last time I saw you was when you were nine." He shook his head.

"Before Malcolm kidnapped me." Her shoulders slumped.

I didn't know if that would ever stop being an issue for her. She'd lost out on so many memories as a child because of it. I pulled her closer to my side and kissed her temple. Things had to work out exactly as they had, or I never would have met her, and we never would have gone on this journey together to save the realms.

"Right," Santori said. "Malcolm. Has anyone taken that bastard's head yet?"

"No." I growled. "But I plan to at the first opportunity."

Santori glanced at me and cocked his head to the side as if confused by what I was doing there. I rolled my shoulders back and stared the Fae down. He was one of the king's friends, but that didn't mean he wouldn't have the same bias as the other Fae.

"You're the Shifter King?" he asked.

"Yes," I said, even though I didn't feel like much of a king as I fought for my life against the Council.

"How did you get to Faery?" It was a general question, not an accusation, and I pulled Aurelia a little closer.

"My mate is incredible." I kissed the top of Aurelia's head.

"Mate? My, things have been happening. Come, I want to hear everything." Santori spun on his heel and barked orders at the people that were now standing around gawking at us.

"Get back to work. We need to be in top shape to defeat the Council!" One of the trainers bellowed as we passed.

"We need your help," Aurelia said at my side. "We have a small army, but it's not enough to defeat the Council. Their actions are unforgivable and must be stopped."

"We have the same goal, Princess. Let's go eat and discuss how we can help each other." Santori grinned as he opened a door that led into more tunnels.

It seemed that everything the rebels did was underground. It would drive my wolf mad to constantly be underground and not feel the sun on my skin. These were dark and dangerous times though, so I could understand the need to hide.

We followed him into the tunnels, to a large dining area. It was empty but could easily seat a hundred men. Santori yelled something, and several women bustled out of the kitchen with platters of food. That was convenient.

"What's been happening here?" the king asked Santori.

"When the Council announced that they'd arrested you for treason, I was suspicious. There was no reason a king would commit treason. A few of your guards were here on leave, and I sought them out. They said that Aurelia had been found and sentenced by the Council to death and you all fled." He eyed our group. "Is that true?"

"Yes, after Ronaldo tortured me to get my powers to ignite." Aurelia crossed her arms.

She hated talking about her time in the castle dungeons, and I knew it wasn't because of the torture. That was where she'd befriended my father, and then he'd died trying to protect her. My father was many things, but that was what I was most grateful to him for. He'd protected my mate when I couldn't.

"We fled and were looking for something to defeat them when Aurelia was sucked down a hole and the rest of us were captured and taken to a human prison to be tortured and killed," the king said. "Aurelia and Asher helped us escape."

Santori eyed Ash. "You're a Rider of the Hunt, yes? Why do you care about what the Council is doing?"

"Faery was once my home too." Ash shrugged, but his body was rigid as if he were expecting a fight. "Despite that, I have alliances to uphold, and the longest running friendship besides my brother's is with Grey. He needs help, and I'm there for him."

"Likewise, brother." I clapped him on the shoulder.

We all dug into the delicious food set before us. I hadn't realized how hungry I was until I'd started eating.

"We somewhat have a plan in place, but we're not sure of anything after gathering allies." Aurelia sat up straighter in her chair.

"And how do you plan to gather allies?" Santori asked with a raised brow.

"We encountered a group of soldiers with blank eyes. They were being controlled by the Council. I was able to remove the mind control, but we suspect that Council has more of the Shadow Warriors controlled the same way. Those warriors are searching for more guards that the Council has under their power so I can remove the control from them as well."

Santori sat back in his chair and gripped his chin between two fingers. "The soldiers only come out to police the people. If you want to find them, you're going to need bait."

I stiffened at his words, not liking the sound of that at all. I glanced at Aurelia at my side and shook my head, already knowing what she was going to propose.

"No. You're not going to be bait." I clenched my hand into a fist.

"Not just me. Isn't there a bounty on all our heads?" She grinned.

"I'll be bait then, and you stay here."

"I can't. I have to be the one to release them from the mind control, Grey." Aurelia crossed her arms and glared at me.

She wasn't wrong, but I couldn't help my need to protect her. She was my mate. I needed her safe. I tilted my head back and squeezed my eyes shut. My wolf was banging against the cage inside my chest.

He wanted to shift and show her who the true alpha was. He wanted to snarl at anyone who got close enough to harm a hair on her head. I took a few calming breaths and pushed him down. His instincts to protect his mate were right, but she didn't see it like that, and I had to try to stop the caveman shit.

"Fine. You glamour yourself like someone from the town, and I'll be bait. He wants me alive to experiment on." I shot her a pleasing look, but I already knew it was no use.

"No, we all act as bait. It's the only way we can explain all the back-up we are going to have when they bring us in." Aurelia shook her head, and I sighed in defeat.

"How many men can you gather to take us to the guards?" I asked Santori.

"There are five of you, so I would think ten would suffice." He shrugged like this was no big deal.

What if something went wrong though? What if this plan didn't actually save anyone, and instead was walking us to our doom?

"It's fine, Grey." Aurelia squeezed my hand. "We will have plenty of back-up, and hopefully free more guards from the Council's mind control."

"But what if we're wrong, and there aren't as many controlled Fae as we think? We could be walking into something we can't get out of," I said. "Ash, Fenrick, what do you think?"

"I think it's risky," Ash said. "I would much rather the princess stay behind, but I understand why she can't. We have to remember they're looking for us as a group and will be suspicious if she's not with us."

I clenched my hand into a fist. I hadn't thought of that. He was right though. The Council would never believe they'd caught us without her. They'd known she was with us when they grabbed us outside the portal.

"Fine. What do we need to do?" I sighed in resignation, hoping I didn't just doom us all with my agreement.

Chapter 13
AURELIA

"IS THIS NECESSARY?" Grey grunted as one of the rebels tied rope around his wrists in front of him.

"They aren't tying it tight. It's just to make the guards think we're under their control." I bumped my shoulder into his.

My hands were already bound in a similar way to Grey as we got ready to make the drop. Well, maybe we weren't making an actual drop, but the Council thought we were being handed over, and that was what really mattered. We needed more warriors, and this was the perfect opportunity to get them.

Santori and his men ushered us through the tunnels to the drop point. We were surrounded by grim faces, though a few sent me nervous glances like they didn't want me to do this. I was their princess and one day queen if we stopped the Council, so I understood the concern.

I had to do this, though. No one else could do it but me. Santori pulled to a stop in front of us and glanced at me over his shoulder.

"Are you ready, You Highness?" he asked.

"As ready as I'll ever be." I shrugged.

"You can still change your mind, love," Grey said, his eyes were pleading with me.

"And do what? Stay behind and let the men fight and probably get captured by the Council? Again." I twisted my arms in the ropes.

They were very loosely tied so I could get out of them easily.

"That was a low blow, love." Grey flinched. "I thought you were dead."

"I'm sorry. I'm just tired of people expecting me to sit back and be the damsel. I'm not the fucking damsel in this story, I'm the hero." I stomped my foot.

Every man in the tunnel stiffened at the loud noise that echoed off the walls. Santori nodded his head then opened the door. Bright sunlight filtered into the tunnel. I took a deep shuddering breath and rolled my shoulders back.

It was time to face the Council guards and hopefully bring them out of their mind control.

We marched through the dark forest silently, surrounded by the rebels. They would shove one of the guys occasionally, just to make it look good.

The canopy of trees blocked out the sun, leaving us in an eerie gloom as we trudged along. Those trees didn't speak to me in the same way as the others in the realm.

"Here!" Santori barked as we came into a clearing.

There was no one there yet, but the guards would be arriving soon, I was sure. Ronaldo wouldn't waste an opportunity to capture us again. We were the biggest threat to him and his plans.

"People are coming," Grey whispered in my ear. "They're trying to surround us."

A man stepped through the trees dressed in the armor of the Council. His eyes glittered with malice and were completely clear of mind control.

"Shit," I whispered. "He's not being controlled."

More men stepped between the trees. There were probably twenty in total, and only half of them had that blank expression I'd seen before.

"Are you sure?" Grey mumbled.

"We can save the ones that are being controlled, but this is going to be bad for Santori and the others." I chewed my lip. "If any of the Council soldiers get away, they will be labeled dissenters."

Ash glanced at me. "Maybe we should make sure none get away then."

Santori stiffened at those words. He didn't like the thought of killing these men any more than I did, but we didn't have a lot of options.

"Let's just take it one step at a time," I said, scanning the group.

The man with the cruel smirk stepped forward and bowed mockingly. "Your Highness, we've been looking for you."

"And why is that? So you can take me back to your master and murder me?" I raised a brow.

My fingers itched to ditch the ropes around my wrists, but I had to time it perfectly. I let the magic build beneath my skin and tingle down my spine.

"You think the Council wants your death? On the contrary. You will be the most prized slave of all once they control your mind." The man laughed.

"I know Ronaldo wants me dead."

"No, not with all that untamed magic running through your veins that he could control. The High Councilor wants you under his thumb."

I glanced between the others as a growl sounded behind me. We needed to stop talking because the overprotective men in my life were all about to lose their shit.

The man just openly admitted to the use of mind control by the Council. Was he stupid, or just overly cocky? Probably both.

I clasped my hands together, and the ropes fell from my wrists. The magic under my skin blasted out of me, seeking the men who were being controlled. They all dropped to the ground, holding their heads, and the man in charge laughed maniacally as he drew his blade.

"I knew this wasn't going to be a simple drop. You think your resistance is secret? Nothing is hidden from the Elders." He swiped his blade at Santori, who jumped back.

Grey released his and the others' hands with the help of his claws and gripped the sword at the belt of the closest rebel. It was exactly as we practiced. Shadows writhed along my skin and mixed with my magic as the men who were controlled blinked rapidly before standing.

They were confused, which was understandable, but we didn't have time to waste. The leader swiped his blade out, and the clang of metal against metal met my ears as Grey faced off with him. A gust of wind blasted through three other guards, throwing them back into the trees on the other side of the clearing.

I turned to Ash and saw he was wielding his sword and his magic at the same time. He winked at me and slashed at his opponent.

"Kill the rest! I need the princess alive!" the asshole fighting Grey bellowed.

My magic exploded out of me as he sliced into Grey's side with his sword. Grey grunted as he stumbled back. Someone was screaming, the shrill tone hurting my ears. It took me a second to realize it was me.

The guards that were previously controlled jumped into action, forming a circle around me, but I shook my head. "Help him. My mate needs your help."

The guards glanced at each other before peering at my father.

"Your Princess gave you a command. Do it!" Father roared.

He was fighting two of the Council's guards at once using his magic and a borrowed sword.

"We need to get out of here!" I yelled.

One of the Shadow Guards we just saved turned in my direction. "Go, Princess, we'll distract them."

I didn't like the sound of that, but with Grey injured, there wasn't much choice. The rebels shouldn't have even been there, but they came to help me. We'd thought it would be easy. I would use my magic on the guards, and they would all fall in line.

We were terribly wrong.

The guards unsheathed their swords in unison and attacked our enemies. The man who stabbed Grey took a step back as the one who spoke lashed out at him.

"What? That's impossible." He scanned the group of Fae that were now on our side with wide eyes and parried another blow from my new friend.

"It's not impossible, and it's the very reason Ronaldo will never control me." I glared at the idiot as I rushed to Grey's side.

The guard lunged at me, and I twirled to the side, throwing shadows in his face as I did. He grunted but he swung again and again.

I didn't have a sword, only the small dagger on my belt that Grey had insisted on. Oh, gods, Grey. I hoped beyond hope he was okay.

Fenrick was next to me in a second. He slashed his sword at the guard, and the man jumped back, a grin plastered on his face.

"The traitor. Your head will bring me power with the Council." He laughed mockingly.

"You have never been a better swordsman than me, Malichai." Fenrick held his borrowed weapon higher.

"No? I think you're remembering things backward. I was chosen for the Council's guard, and you were chosen to babysit a princess." Malichai laughed.

"I was chosen for the highest honor of guarding our future monarch while you were nothing but a cog in a corrupt machine. You were a grunt, chosen to do the Council's dirty work," Fenrick snarled.

I glanced over at Ash, who was still battling a guard when two of the warriors I'd saved rushed to intercept the guard attacking him.

"What are we going to do, Princess?"

"We need to get out of here." I leaned down to inspect Grey's wound.

Something didn't look quite right about the stab wound. I peered at Grey, but his skin was ashen, and his breath rattled in his chest. I ran my fingers over his face, and he blinked up at me in confusion.

"Go. You need to go without me." He coughed.

"No," I said. "I'm not leaving you behind."

He leaned up on his elbows and tried to roll to his knees, but I pushed him back down. Fenrick stood at my back, the clash of swords clanging in my ears. What was going to happen if I didn't do something quickly?

All the Council guards were fighting with the Shadow Warriors I'd freed from the mind control, and Santori's men formed a wall around us. Two men rushed forward and picked Grey up gentler than I would have thought possible for trained warriors.

"We can't go back to base. If they follow us, then we will doom everyone." Santori stepped forward.

"Agreed. We have a place, but sifting is still difficult for me, and I'm afraid with his injuries it will be too much." I wrung my hands together as I stared at my mate.

"Go, Princess!" one of the warriors shouted. "We'll hold them off."

"Do you know which way to the house?" I asked Fenrick.

"Yes." He nodded.

"Let's go." I waved a hand for him to lead us back to the house.

It wouldn't hold everyone for long, but we could get away from the assholes trying to kill us. We followed behind Fenrick, and I prayed to whatever gods might be listening that the men we left behind would be okay.

I had others to worry about, though. I had to worry about the realms and my mate. He couldn't leave me now, just when we were coming to the end of this war. I needed him. I glanced at him, and his eyes bored into mine.

"You should have left me behind, my love. I am nothing but a burden right now."

"Stop it. We aren't leaving you behind, you self-sacrificing idiot." I threw my hands up.

"Why the fuck would we leave you behind?" Asher roared and shook his head.

"I'm only slowing you down," Grey rasped.

"Shut up," Fenrick growled and stomped ahead.

"I don't care if you slow us down. We will fight if we need to. I refuse to let you die out here. It's you and me against the world, remember?" I rushed to catch up with Fenrick.

I couldn't take another word of Grey's self-sacrificing bullshit. I needed him just like he needed me. I was pretty sure I'd proven that again and again.

I would prove it a million times over, as long as it meant he was sitting safely by my side.

The only problem was that no one was safe. Even if we got back to the house in time, something wasn't right, and I had a feeling nothing ever would be again.

Chapter 14

GREY

THEY WERE BEING unreasonable as we trudged through the dark forest. They needed to sift back to the house to flee the Council, but Aurelia refused to sift because it might be too much for me in my current condition.

"Leave me behind!" I demanded, but they had all stopped listening about ten minutes ago.

Aurelia didn't even turn at my demand. Her shoulders stiffened, but she continued to stomp forward.

"Maybe we should just knock him out. His hollering to be left behind is probably bringing attention we don't want." Santori chuckled.

"No one hurts my mate," Aurelia said with a growl.

"He's being a pain in the ass," Santori mumbled, but my oversensitive hearing picked up on the words.

"I don't care. Ignore him." She glared at me over her shoulder. "No one is leaving you behind. It's not an option, so stop it."

"You would already be safe at the house if you had." I narrowed my eyes at her.

This wound wasn't healing, and I didn't know how much time I had left. It would kill Aurelia to watch me die. I couldn't stand that.

"We're almost there, Grey. Stop with the bullshit!" Fenrick barked.

I growled from my spot flung over the rebel's arm like a sack of flour. I hated being weak, but I couldn't deny that the pain was visceral, and every second on this man's shoulder, pain sliced through me. The wound had stopped bleeding quickly, but it still wasn't healing.

There was something terribly wrong, and I didn't want my mate to watch me die from a Council guard's blade. The wound wasn't closing but rather turning an ugly shade of greenish black. I expected poison, but I couldn't be sure. It had been centuries since I'd been back to Faery, and anything could have been developed by the Fae since then.

I was carried across the tree line, and we stopped outside the wards to the house where we were staying. I groaned as we walked across the wards and a thousand fire ants lit me up from the inside out. It wasn't actually fire ants, but the effects the wards had on me as I passed.

I stopped arguing as I was carried into the house to the bedroom Aurelia and I had shared. No one but the man who carried me and my friends followed inside. Aurelia wrung her hands as I was laid on the bed. I reached a weak arm out to her, and she sat on the edge of the mattress next to my hip.

"What's wrong? Why isn't he healing?" she asked.

The king stepped forward and bent at the waist to check the wound. His expression turned grim.

"You knew?" the king snarled.

"I had an idea, yes," I said glancing at the wall.

The accusing stare was too much. He knew as well as I did that there was only one way to stop this poison coursing through my body.

"That's why you were so adamant about being left behind." He crossed his arms over his chest.

"What's going on? What aren't you telling me?" Aurelia asked.

Tears pooled in her eyes, and she placed her hands over the wound on my chest. A green glow lit her palms as her power rushed through me. She was wasting her energy. I reached for her hands, but she batted mine away and kept pushing more magic into me.

"Aurelia, stop," I whispered.

"Fenrick, help me," she said, turning to the Fae guardian.

"You're the strongest of us, Princess. If you can't do it, then I won't be able to either." He hung his head.

"No, I don't accept that. What is wrong with him?" Aurelia turned pleading eyes to her father.

The king stared at me, and I begged him with my eyes not to put this on her. I didn't want it to be like this. Why couldn't the Fates give me just one good thing that wasn't shrouded in sadness?

"The blade had poison on it, Aurelia. A poison that is resistant to healing magic. That's why he's not healing," he said, glancing down at the blackened wound.

"Poison? What kind of poison? How do we cure it? There has to be a way to save him." She jumped to her feet and paced.

"No," I said. "Let me go. You can be happy again after you defeat the Council. I don't want it to be this way."

I reached for her hand and pulled her back down on the bed next to me. She only resisted a little bit, finally sitting down and glaring at every man in the room.

"Someone better tell me right now how to fix this." Her gaze landed on mine.

Tears stained her cheeks as they slid down in rivers. I reached up, wiping them away as my chest burned with agony. She was crying, and this would destroy her. Was I being selfish not to tell her the only known antidote to the poison?

"I've only ever heard rumors about this working and there's a cost involved." The king glanced at me. "Doing this could put your life at risk as well, daughter."

"I don't care. I will do anything to save him. Tell me what I must do." She squeezed my hand.

"It's all just rumors and speculation but from what I have heard, the blood of a Fae is the only way to heal that poison. He would have to bite you and tie himself to you in a completed mate bond."

"I won't do it. Not like this," I growled.

"It will save your stubborn ass." Aurelia threw her hands up in frustration.

"We don't know that," I growled. "He also didn't tell you this risk. If this rumor isn't true and your blood can't save me, then you will die with me. Everything will be for nothing if you die, and the Council enslaves everyone."

I winced as the blackness on my stomach spread a little more. Pain rushed through me, but the pain in my heart was worse. My chest cracked open at the thought of leaving Aurelia behind, but that was the fate I was dealt.

"I don't care!" she screamed. "I will not lose you. Let the fucking world burn for all I care."

Her shadows pulsed and writhed angrily on her arms as she stared me down with a fire I didn't know she was capable of. In that moment, I saw her for who she could have been if the Council and Malcolm hadn't gotten away with her kidnapping. She was fierce and angry, and would let the Council burn the world to the ground.

"Aurelia, think about this," Fenrick whispered.

"I have thought about it." She rolled her shoulders back and pinned him with her stare.

"I don't want to live in a world without him in it. Is that selfish? Maybe, but I have been running around the realms trying to stop the Council for everyone else. Grey is mine. I think I'm allowed to be selfish this once."

Fenrick's shoulders slumped in defeat. He knew as well as I did that she wasn't going to budge on this. She called me stubborn, but she was even more stubborn than I was when she got something in her head.

"She's not wrong," Ash spoke for the first time. "If anyone can survive this, it's the princess. You said yourself, Fenrick, she's the strongest of us all."

"See? I can do this. I can heal him. As long as *he* does what *he's* supposed to." She glared at me.

"It's not a risk I'm willing to take. You're meant to be queen. You're meant to save the supernaturals, and usher in a new era for all supernaturals. You can't do that if you're dead." I flinched in pain as I shifted on the bed.

"Everyone out," Aurelia whispered. "He won't do this with everyone here."

"I won't do this at all, so they might as well stay."

"Get! Out!" Aurelia roared.

I shook my head, but the others still stepped out of the room, closing the door firmly behind them. The traitors. Though, I probably would have done the same if that anger had been directed at me.

"You will do this, Grey." She clenched her fists at her sides.

"No."

"If you don't, I'll follow you right into the beyond. I will let the world burn." She placed her palm on my chest over my heart.

My wolf was eerily silent through the entire argument. He didn't really understand what was happening, or why he was so weak. It was more of an impression in my mind than an actual feeling.

"You wouldn't let everything be destroyed, my love. I know you're a better person than that." I shook my head and placed my hand over hers on my heart.

"Please, Grey. Don't make me live without you. Try, please?" she cried.

Pain, sadness and anger warred inside of me that it was coming to this. Aurelia leaned her head down on my shoulder, her hot tears dropping on me, but I didn't dare wipe them away.

If the roles were reversed, would I be begging her the same? I would do anything to keep her safe and in my arms, and I was denying her that same right.

But I wasn't the one who was meant to change the world. She was. If she died, all would be lost. We would be in the beyond together though, and we wouldn't have to live in the world without each other.

My own selfish desires were warring with my need to fix this world, and the longer she sobbed over me, the harder they were to fight.

"I didn't want our actual mating to be in a time of sadness, of a desperate need to save me," I whispered and wrapped my arm around her.

"We won't have a mating at all if you don't stop being so bullheaded." She sniffed.

I chuckled and then groaned as the pain seared through me. It was getting worse. I was getting weaker. If I didn't make a decision soon, I wouldn't be able to.

"Okay," I said, and her head shot up from my shoulder. "I'll do it."

"This will work, Grey. It has to." She grinned.

Aurelia helped me to sit up in the bed, and I winced at the black marks crawling up my abs to my heart. She pushed her hair away from her neck and tilted her head to the side, offering me everything in that one moment. This selfless, beautiful, perfect woman was mine, and providing me another chance to try to prove I was worthy of her.

I wasn't worthy of her, but every second I breathed, I was going to do my best to show her how truly perfect she was, and that she was mine.

I kissed her neck in the spot where I intended to claim her l. My mate gasped at the contact but only leaned in closer to me.

"I love you, Grey. Please, make me yours for eternity," she whispered.

My wolf howled in my head. It was the first noise he'd made since I'd been stabbed, and my teeth elongated in my mouth. I kissed her neck again, hoping I didn't hurt her when I claimed her as mine.

Aurelia fisted the sheets at my sides as my teeth grazed her skin not in a bite but a tease. I needed her to relax. This was meant to be euphoric, but since we were in a dire situation, I wasn't sure how it would go.

I prayed to whatever gods might be listening that I wasn't about to doom the world as I sank my fangs into her neck.

Chapter 15
AURELIA

AS GREY PLUNGED his teeth into my skin, I screamed. White-hot euphoria blasted through me, and rainbows danced behind my eyes. I didn't understand how anything that felt this good could have inspired such fear in my mate.

He truly was my mate now. The bond snapped into place in my chest, and my body shook with pleasure. "Grey."

He pulled back and licked at my neck with a groan. I blinked away the fog in my brain and grinned at him. "We're linked."

"We are, and we didn't die." He glanced down at the stab wound but it was already knitting itself back together.

"You're healing," I said.

I reached for him and ran my hand over the healing skin. It was rejuvenating at an amazing speed.

"You don't usually recover that quickly," I said with awe.

"I took on some of your healing abilities." Grey brushed my hair out of my eyes and leaned forward, kissing me hungrily. "You are truly perfect."

"I told you this would work."

Grey wrapped his arms around me and pulled me into his chest. "Yes, you're apparently smarter than me too."

"I'm glad you're seeing that now." I giggled.

Grey cupped my cheek and kissed me again, not waiting a second before he was seeking entrance to my mouth. I pulled back and frowned at him.

"You're still healing. You nearly died. We can't do that right now." I shook my head.

"It's part of the bonding, love." He kissed down my throat over the mark he'd just left on my skin.

I shuddered under his touch.

"We can't," I groaned.

Grey ignored me as he rolled us, so he was pinning me to the bed. "I need you. Now."

He ripped my shirt over my head with a growl of hunger and tweaked a nipple through the fabric of my bra. I wiggled my hips even as I tried for a third time to slow down. He wasn't having any of it.

His claw retracted from his hand, and he sliced through the thin material between my breasts as if it were butter. He flung the scraps off the bed and attacked my breasts, sucking my nipple into his mouth and between his teeth.

My back arched, pressing into his mouth even higher. Grey growled against me, sending tingles dancing over my skin. My fingers ran through silky hair, pulling him down closer instead of pushing him away.

"I can't wait another second to taste you, sweet mate." He licked down my stomach to my jeans and growled.

"I didn't exactly have time to get undressed." I reached between us.

Grey slapped my hands away. "I'll do it."

"Don't rip." I stopped when he did exactly that.

The sound of ripping fabric tore through the room, and I flinched. He was tearing all my clothes and I wouldn't have any left.

"Grey, I'm not going to have anything else to wear," I groaned, but he wasn't listening to me as he spread my legs wider.

He picked up my calf using the back of my knee, and I shivered as he placed a kiss there before moving higher. Grey's eyes glowed with his wolf as he watched me. He licked my inner thigh, and I squirmed, wiggling my hips. I needed something. I needed him.

"I needed you naked." His gaze roamed over me.

My chest heaved as he leaned down and inhaled deeply through his nose. What the hell was he doing? Was he smelling me?

"Mine," he growled and licked his lips.

He was more wolf than man. Was his wolf taking control? All thoughts fled as he licked all the way up my slit and circled my clit. My back arched and my fingers dug into his scalp.

"Grey!" I shouted to the ceiling, my head thrashing.

He just circled my clit faster before sucking it into his mouth. His fingers dug into my inner thighs, holding them spread wide. I bucked up into his mouth, and his gaze found mine. The glow of his eyes brightened further.

Lips and teeth and tongue ate at me savagely, and my hands tightened further in his hair. My spine tingled with the beginnings of my orgasm and my body shook with tremors. I didn't know how much longer I could last with the way he was devouring me. He growled against me, and my hips bucked.

"Not yet, mate. You will come again when I'm buried inside you." Grey backed away from me.

A strangled groan escaped my lips as I realized what he was doing. He was edging me.

"Then fuck me already and seal the mate bond." I gripped his shoulders with a strength I didn't know I had and pulled him closer.

Grey fell over me, but his hands snapped out on either side, keeping him from crushing me with his weight. He leaned down and took my lips with his. I kissed him hard, tasting myself on his tongue. My hips bucked against him, but Grey just chuckled into my mouth.

"You're a needy little thing, aren't you, mate?" he whispered against my lips.

He tweaked my nipple between his fingers before running his hand down over my belly and pushed two fingers inside me. My body clenched around those fingers as he curled them inside me, hitting that part of me that set off my orgasm.

"Grey!" I shouted as fire tore through my veins.

My whole body shook with my release as white filled my vision. Grey chuckled and continued thrusting his fingers inside me hard and fast, prolonging the orgasm as he kissed my neck where his mate mark sat on my skin.

"I need you to mark me, mate," he groaned. "I need your mark on my skin more than I need breath in my body. Make me yours."

"I'm not a wolf, Grey. I don't know how to do that," I said as I came down from the high I was on.

"It's an instinct, my love. Do what feels natural to you." He rolled to his back and pulled me with him, so I was on top. "The bond won't be fully formed until you do."

I straddled his waist and stared down at him. He was already mine, but how did I mark him to prove it to the world? I didn't really care about proving it to anyone else but with the way Grey was staring at me, he needed this more than anything in the world.

I had to think of a way to mark him even if I couldn't shift my teeth and bite him like he'd done to me. I reached between us and gripped his cock in my hand, pumping him slowly and methodically while I searched my instincts for a way to mark him.

Grey gripped my wrist and moaned as he pulled my hand away and wrapped it around his throat. "I know my cock belongs to you, love, but I would rather you mark me for the world to see. I'm yours for eternity."

"I'm yours as well, mate." I leaned down and kissed his lips.

My hand around his neck tingled as I scooted further down his body. His other hand tightened on my hip. "I'm the luckiest man in the world, but I won't be able to hold myself back from flipping you over and fucking you until you're screaming for me."

"Why would you want to hold yourself back?" I asked with a grin.

My hand on his neck heated as I shimmied down his body. I lined my entrance up with his cock and grinned as I rubbed myself against him. A strangled moan escaped Grey as I wiggled my hips. He hissed as golden light seeped from my hand around his throat.

"What's happening?" I asked as I sat up and sank myself down on his huge cock.

"It feels like fire, but in the best possible way," he said, breathless. "I think you're marking me, mate."

"How?" I groaned as the light grew brighter and I circled my hips.

His cock hit that spot inside me, and I screamed just as the light beneath my palm nearly blinded me. Grey reached up, holding my hips down so he could buck his hips up into mine.

"Come for me, mate. Seal the mate bond for eternity!" he yelled.

I came again, and my whole body trembled as my hand that had been fused to his neck only moments before finally dimmed. I removed my hand as I collapsed on his chest with panting breaths as the aftershocks of my orgasm continued to tear through me.

The golden cord that had formed between us strengthened as I stared at his neck, where a dark black blotch that looked like the humans' depiction of a fairy was etched into his skin. That was my mark. I trailed my fingers over the blackened skin, and he groaned even as he was spent.

"What does it look like?" he rasped as he pulled me down.

"It's a black fairy. Like a Shadow Fae." I smiled.

"Perfect." He grinned back at me and pulled me to his side.

I laid my head on his chest, listening closely to the strong beat of his heart. He was here, and we were connected. I didn't have to worry about him dying.

"We should probably get up and do something." I shifted, but his arm banded tighter around me.

"Not yet," he whispered and kissed my forehead. "I'm not quite ready to face the world yet after our mating."

I glanced up at him with a frown. "What does this bond mean for us? You healed faster than ever."

"I don't exactly know what it means. There will be changes in both of us in the coming days and weeks." He peered down at me with so much adoration in his eyes that my heart swelled with love for the man holding me.

He was worth the risk. I wished he realized that more than he did. I never wanted to have another argument like that again. He believed in his own mind that risking everything for me was acceptable, but me doing the same was not.

"I hope you understand now that we are in this together, no matter what, if you can risk your life for me, then I can do the same for you." I poked him in the chest.

"You are literally the only hope to save the realms. Excuse me if I don't want to jeopardize that along with your life when we both owe Ronaldo a gruesome final death." He rubbed my back as he spoke.

I understood where he was coming from because we were fighting a war against oppression, but how good would that victory actually feel if I didn't have him there to share it with me?

"I don't care about anything if you're not there to share in the victory." I kissed his chest over his heart. "We're in this together, Grey. For eternity."

"No more making decisions without consulting each other. I will try to contain my wolf instincts as long as we can try to come to a mutual agreement where your safety is concerned."

"We're linked now, Grey. Our life forces are tied together, so your safety matters just as much as mine." He opened his mouth to protest, but my hand covered his mouth. "No arguments. I know you feel the connection as strongly as I do. If something were to happen to you, I would die too. No more risks for either of us. We need to be smart if we're going to win this war."

"Fine. But there's no way in this realm or any other that I won't always worry about your safety. I will protect you with my last breath," Grey said. "Even if that means it's yours as well."

Chapter 16

GREY

"I THINK it's time to go back," Aurelia announced to the others. "We need to start planning for war."

Santori ran a hand over his face. "Are your supernaturals ready for war?"

"They're some of the best trained fighters I've ever seen." I nodded.

Some of those people had been with me since I opened the Syndicate. They had been training for centuries to take down the Council. They were ready. They had to be.

"What about your people?" Aurelia asked. "I saw many just learning how to use shadow magic."

"When the time comes, the rebels will use whatever they have at their disposal to take down the Council," Santori said.

Fenrick leaned forward in his seat, eyeing us all. "Are we sure about this?"

"What do you mean?" I asked. "We don't have a choice but to take them down."

"No, no. That's not what I'm asking. I'm just wondering if we are moving too quickly. We only have one shot at taking down the Council, and I don't want to blow it because we weren't prepared."

"We're ready, and I think we need to move before any of their experiments are successful.. Their mind control doesn't work on shifters currently. What if they figure it out though? They could take over half our army during battle and then all would be lost."

"What about the rest of the controlled warriors?" Fenrick drummed his fingers on the arm of his chair.

"They will be freed as soon as the Council is gone. They might already be on to the fact that I can free their guards," Aurelia said.

"It depends on the possibility the mind-controlled guards that fought against those assholes in the forest let any of them get away. We have to operate under the assumption that the Council knows what you can do." I squeezed Aurelia's hip.

"Okay, then, when do you leave and how will you contact us?" Santori asked.

The man was obviously ready for a fight. I didn't blame him. After seeing for myself the destruction the Council was bringing to the Fae, I was ready for this battle as well. I glanced at my mate, and nervousness tore through our bond.

What would happen to us during this war? War was violent and there was never a real winner. People were lost on both sides, and lives were changed forever. We were fighting for survival, though. Not just our own, but that of the entire supernatural population of the realms.

"We will leave as soon as possible, and if you could allow Fenrick access to sift into the tunnels, he will send words when it's time to fight." Aurelia sat up straighter in her chair.

Her posture was rigid and regal. She looked every inch the queen she would one day become. Her doubts trickled into the bond, and I glanced over, flexing my fingers on her hip to get her attention. She peered at me with a small smile as I poured all my confidence in her and our armies into the bond.

"I'll make it so the wards will accept Fenrick," Santori agreed with a nod.

"Okay, I guess it's time to go back and rally everyone together." I stood, pulling Aurelia up at my side.

I never liked going back to the human world once I'd been in Faery, but hopefully once we defeated the Council, that wouldn't be an issue. I scanned the house, imagining a whole different life for myself and my mate. One where we could make the place a home. It wasn't realistic. We were both royals, and the house wasn't well defended, but it would still be ours.

Fenrick clapped us both on the shoulders and grinned. "Ready to get back?"

"Let's go. The faster we do this, the faster we can end the Council for good."

We swirled through time and space, and the landing wasn't as difficult this time as my feet crunched the gravel as I touched down. Aurelia didn't even stumble this time. Were we just getting used to sifting, or was it the bond that made things easier? I was stronger now, and power thrummed beneath my skin, but I didn't dare use it until I knew what it did.

We landed outside the wards, but I stepped in front of Aurelia at the scene that played out before me. The wards to the building were surrounded by the human military. Guns were drawn when they caught sight of us, and blank eyes stared us down.

"Fuck. We're in trouble," I mumbled as Malcolm stepped out from the crowd.

"I can save them the same way I did the Fae guards," Aurelia whispered behind me.

She didn't move to stand next to me. I was grateful for that. She was letting me protect her.

"They're just humans. What if you break their minds?" I asked.

Even the Fae had been affected by her breaking the control on their minds. It wasn't painless.

"What else can we do?" she asked. "We're greatly outnumbered."

Ash and the Shadow King stepped up next to me with their swords drawn. "We're going to have to fight and let Aurelia at least try."

"Malcolm is mine," I growled.

Aurelia spun me toward her and kissed me hard. "I'm going to try to break the control and then race across the wards to get help."

"That's a good plan." I nodded and turned back to the humans.

If Dan grabbed some of the others who were trained to fight, then we could even the odds a bit. How long had they been outside my wards, waiting to ambush my people?

"Malcolm!" I roared. "Fight me."

"Why would I do that when I could just have the humans kill you and bring the princess with me?" Malcolm planted his hands on his hips.

"You mean my bonded mate?" I asked with a grin.

Malcolm's expression became murderous as his face turned red.

"You lie." Malcolm unsheathed his sword.

"Why would I lie about that?" I crouched into a fighting stance.

He stalked forward, his face turning almost purple with rage. "You would lie to get out of death. You think I won't kill you if it means her death."

He slashed his sword at me, and I jumped back, bringing up my own weapon to block the blow. We were evenly matched. We'd fought several times before, and the slippery bastard had always gotten away.

I lunged forward and sliced at his midsection, but the clang of his sword meeting mine filled the air. Magic bubbled up inside me, begging me to unleash it. I didn't know how to use magic. I was a shifter, and the only thing I'd ever learned to do was shift.

Malcolm swung his blade, and I parried with my own as static electricity crawled up my arms and tingled at my fingertips. The sword glowed blue with power, and I swiped out at Malcolm again.

The electricity hit his blade and he yelped, dropping the weapon. The scent of charred flesh burned in my nose as he glanced down at his blackened hand.

"You really did bond with the princess," he said, and his good hand pooled with magic.

Fuck. He was going to fight with magic now. I didn't even know how I'd done that with the sword. The magic had a life of its own. I gripped the sword in both hands, unsure what I was going to do now as more and more magic built in his palm.

"I told you I had. You're the one who didn't want to believe it." I shrugged with a nonchalance I didn't feel.

He threw the ball of magic at me with a battle cry, and I swung the blade at it, running on instinct alone. When the magic connected with the blade, it bounced off and hit Malcolm square in the chest.

Malcolm screamed as his own magic burned a hole through his chest and he dropped to his knees. I stalked forward with my blade.

"I told you, one day I would have your head." I swung the sword still crackling with magic in a wide arc and his head tumbled from his shoulders and rolled away.

The humans all stopped battling with the supernaturals that Aurelia had gotten to help and blinked at each other in confusion. I scanned the battlefield, only caring about finding one person.

Aurelia was several feet from the wards, squaring off with a human who stopped and blinked at her. She held her magic back at the last second before spinning on her heel. A brilliant smile lit up her face with relief and pride when she glanced at the body at my feet.

"You did it!" she yelled and ran into my arms. "He's finally gone."

"Aurelia!" the king bellowed, and I spun just in time to shield her from the man that rushed us.

"What did you do to us?" the man shouted.

He held his gun at the ready, with his finger on the trigger, willing to take us out if necessary. Aurelia squared her shoulders and rose up to her full height as she stared the human down.

"We did nothing but save you from being controlled by that monster."

"You're all monsters. That man was helping us round up all of you." This soldier had obviously been drinking Kool-Aid before his mind had been controlled.

"These *monsters* have been living among humans for centuries, and you never knew it. They have been your neighbors or possibly even friends, and you turn on them so easily because they were born with magic?" Aurelia said.

"They were biding their time, waiting to enslave humans," the soldier said.

I scoffed. "Yeah, because we sat back and waited for human technology that could literally destroy the world before we were ready to attack you and take you out. We watched the human population grow to an unimaginable size that outnumbered us a hundred to one before we decided it was time. Do you even hear yourself right now?"

"He's completely brainwashed, Grey. There's no reasoning with him." Aurelia turned to Dan. "Lock him in the cells. He's a danger to us."

"Are we sure that arresting human soldiers is the best idea, love?" I asked but nodded to Dan to do as she said.

Dan stepped closer, but the man swung the butt of his rifle straight for Dan's head. His reflexes kicked in at the last second, and he gripped the gun, tossing it to the side and tackled the man. More soldiers raced forward, but the majority hung back to see what was going to happen.

They weren't shooting at us, so we had an advantage. One man raced toward Aurelia, but before he could get there, magic buzzed beneath my skin and suddenly, without taking a step, I was in front of her, blocking the blow of the weapon with my forearm.

I reached up and ripped the gun from his hand and turned it on him, hitting him in the face. He crumpled to the ground.

"Grey, did you just sift?" Aurelia whispered behind me.

I glanced at her with a smirk. "I think I did."

I turned back to the chaos. All the men who'd rushed us were being carted away by my team. The other humans still stood around with a mixture of awe and trepidation.

"We are no threat to you. The Fae who have wormed their way into your government are the real threat. All we want is peace," Aurelia called to the soldiers still standing around appearing confused.

A man dressed in all black tactical gear stepped forward and glanced at Malcolm's headless body with a frown. "We can't have peace. Now that supernaturals are known to the world, I fear there will never be peace between us."

It was the same fear I'd had for centuries. It was why we'd worked so hard to stay hidden. As long as we were in the human realm, no supernatural would ever be safe.

Chapter 17

AURELIA

THE SOLDIERS MILLED around the battlefield outside the ward. Most had no memory of anything that had happened in the last few weeks. How could the Council control them so thoroughly that their memories were wiped clean?

"Are we sure letting them go is a good idea?" Ash asked. "What if they lead the government right to us?"

"The troublemakers are in the cells now, Ash. I can't hold the human army in prison because we're scared."

"She's right. They will see it as an act of war," Grey said.

He wrapped his arm around me. We hadn't had a chance yet to talk about the new powers he was displaying. He'd sifted right in front of me. I hadn't even learned to control that particular power yet. It only worked when my emotions were high.

"We don't need a war with the humans." I sighed. "Once we defeat the Council, everyone can return to Faery and leave the humans alone."

"It won't end there, love. The humans know we exist now. They will always be looking for us." Grey pulled me in close.

The soldiers wandered away in groups, speaking frantically to each other in hushed tones, but at least they were leaving. All except the man in the tactical gear who'd spoken before. He stepped up to me with a nod.

"You're the princess everyone is looking for," he said.

"I am."

"I remember more than the others. I am a Secret Service agent. I'm not even supposed to be working with the army." He shook his head.

"You were at the gala." Grey narrowed his eyes on the man.

"Yes, I don't remember everything, but most of it. I have some information you might need. Is there somewhere private we can talk?" the man asked.

I glanced at the building, unsure if I should even suggest it. He'd been the one to say we would never have peace, but now he was asking for a private place to give us intel? I wasn't sure if that was the best idea.

"Why should we trust you?" Grey asked. "You said yourself that we will never have peace."

"The information I have is what you want, and I'm risking everything, including my life, to give it to you. I can't talk out in the open like this." He scanned the clearing, but all the soldiers had already left.

"How important is this information?" I asked. "Is it life or death?"

"It could be, for a lot of people." The man glanced between us.

I didn't know if we could trust him, but he was sticking his neck on the chopping block just having the conversation with us. What if he left and that intel could have ended the war in our favor?

"I think we should go inside, Grey. We should hear him out." I chewed my lip.

"Fine, but I hope you understand we'll need to take your weapons and you will be guarded the entire time you're inside the wards." Grey stepped forward, waving a hand.

Dan and two other shifters stepped around the man.

"I understand." The man held his arms up.

"Search him. Take any weapons he has, or any kind of listening devices, and then we'll step into the building." Grey said to Dan.

The man had an impressive arsenal of weapons strapped to his body. It was a little terrifying. I never would have checked some of the places where they'd found guns and knives.

"Take off your boots," Dan ordered.

He untied the laces and took them off one at a time. Dan pulled two small daggers and a handgun out of each.

"They have compartments in the heels," the man told Dan and clicked a button.

A blade shot from the back of the heel of the boot, and I gasped. Dan wrenched it out of the heel and handed the boot back to the man before doing the same with the other.

"These aren't standard military-issue," Dan grunted.

I counted fifteen weapons pulled from various places on the man's body, but they found no listening devices.

"Use your magic, Dan," Grey commanded.

"What magic?" I asked as Dan's hands glowed a midnight blue.

"He can detect and disable electronics. So if there were any hidden devices on him, they won't be recording anymore." Grey crossed his arms over his chest.

"I told him where the blades in my boots were. Why would I do that if I was hiding listening devices?" He shook his head.

"You may not even know they're hidden on you. You were being mind controlled, remember," I said.

He nodded and allowed Dan to continue his search.

"I found something," Dan said with a growl. "It doesn't matter now, though, it's fried."

"Let's go." I stomped forward.

I was too curious for my own good. What information did he have for us, and why would he give it to us in the first place? He was Secret Service, and the President wasn't the biggest fan of supernaturals. My shoulders slumped as I followed them to the garage. It was hard to think about the gala. We'd lost Zeke that night and had to leave him behind.

We all got into the elevator and Grey pushed the button for the interrogation floor. That was on the same floor we'd just had all the horrible humans sent.

"Are you sure that's a good idea?" I asked.

"We need to make it look like he's on their side, and we're locking him up too. They will all be released to the authorities once we get a witch to wipe the memory of our location from their minds." Grey grasped my hand.

"You have a tactical mind." The man nodded. "I appreciate you taking those steps to protect my life."

"Like I said before, we aren't the monsters we've been made out to be." I shuffled my feet as I waited for the ding of the elevator.

The wait was torturous, even though it was probably only a minute. The elevator doors finally opened, and Dan shoved the man out into the room. Magical cells lined the walls, and Lydia screamed obscenities at us. It was just another day at the Syndicate.

"You can't leave me in here with humans!" Lydia yelled.

"You're lucky I didn't put any in the cell with you," Dan barked. "Now shut up before I cut your rations."

Lydia closed her mouth and sat back against the wall, glaring at us. Well, she was glaring at me, as usual. She hated me after what happened when I'd first came to the syndicate. She and Grey's second-in-command had done some shady dealings with Malcolm to get rid of me. She deserved to be locked up.

"Don't bother with her. I forgot she was even here." Grey waved a hand as we continued past the cells. "Put him in the box. I need to have a chat."

Grey glared at the men in the cells as he walked past them. They had attacked us of their own free will. They thought we were monsters, but they were. They were the ones rounding up supernaturals and persecuting them for being different. Had they learned nothing from their own history?

Apparently not.

We followed Dan into the box with the Secret Service agent. It was a twelve-by-twelve room with no windows. It had a single metal table in the middle of the room that was bolted to the floor. I closed the door behind us with a soft click and turned to the agent.

"This is the most secure place in the building besides my floor.

You can speak freely here." Grey sat in the chair in front of the table and pulled me down on his lap.

"You're the ones who've been rescuing the supernaturals from the prisons and the intake facilities," he said, if wasn't a question.

"Yes," I said. "Why is that important?"

"There's a secret facility that no one but the President and a few top advisors know about."

"We haven't been able to get to all of them yet." My shoulders slumped.

I wanted to get everyone out of all of them, but there wasn't space here, and we had to gather an army. The fact that so many supernaturals were still being tested weighed me down.

"This place isn't on any list you may have. It's top-secret. Only for the high profile supernaturals that the high Councilor wants for special projects."

"And why are you telling us this?" Grey asked.

"You said you have been breaking in and getting people out. I'm giving you the top-secret location of one of these places to do just that." The man sounded frustrated as he growled the last word.

"You lost someone." I cocked my head to the side.

"My wife is a witch. They somehow figured it out and detained her and my nineteen-year-old daughter. They have been holding them there over my head, so I'll do their bidding." He rubbed his eyes.

I glanced away from him. He was emotional, and I didn't think he would appreciate my sympathy.

"I'm sorry about your wife and daughter, but we have a war on the horizon and more people here than we can deal with. Once we beat the Council, we'll try to get everyone out of those facilities and make a treaty with the President, but until then, we are spread too thin." I hung my head.

Tears clogged my throat and burned the back of my eyes. I hated leaving people in those facilities even a day longer than they needed to be.

"You don't understand. I'm not just asking for them. There's someone you love there as well." His eyes bored into mine.

"What are you talking about?" I sat forward on Grey's lap with a frown.

"The man with you at the gala. The one who was shot. He didn't die from that gunshot wound. He's still alive."

Ash's fist slammed into the man's shoulder, toppling him over in his chair. The guy grunted but didn't fight back. He raised his hands in surrender.

"You think you can get us to save your family faster by lying to us?" Ash growled low and threatening.

He leaned over the man with a snarl before Dan clapped him on the shoulder.

"Ease up. There are ways to find out if he's lying, man," Dan said.

Ash straightened to his full height. His body was rigid, and his expression contorted with rage.

"I'm not lying. I was ordered to stay with the President after you all fled, and what I saw was a bit terrifying. The man who was shot laid there bleeding, but a few minutes later, the bullet popped loose from his side and the skin healed. I was forced to knock him out again and they took him out through the back."

My eyes widened, and hope flared inside me. Could it really be true? Could Zeke really be alive? I glanced at Grey, but he was staring intently at the man.

"How do you know he wasn't taken to a different facility?" Grey asked.

"Malcolm ordered them to take him to the secret facility. He's there with my wife and daughter." He stood and brushed off his clothes.

"Zeke's alive," Ash said softly.

His gaze met mine across the room, and a grin tugged at my lips. "Where is this facility, and how do we get them out?"

He wrote down coordinates and handed them to Grey, but his expression was still grim. "One last thing. You need to hurry, because Ronaldo almost has his mind control serum perfected. Once he does, they will be the first he uses it on."

We were fighting against a clock again. Why couldn't anything ever be simple?

Chapter 18

GREY

"**THIS COULD BE A TRAP,**" I said once we were back in my office, away from prying ears.

"He dropped a bomb on us... was it so we would hurry up and free his family? We can't let the Council complete their serum." Dan ran a hand down his face.

Fenrick pulled Zeke's laptop closer and powered it on, gripping the coordinates in his other hand. How did we even know if the place existed? The guy could have been lying through his teeth about everything to lure us to the government.

"If Zeke's alive, we have to do something," Aurelia said.

She held an insane amount of guilt bottled up inside for what had happened to Zeke. I wished I could take it away or soothe it somehow.

"It's in the Nevada desert, but there's nothing there. Just sand." Fenrick frowned at the screen.

"Could they have them in a bunker of some kind?" Ash leaned over Fenrick's shoulder.

"It's possible." Fenrick clicked a couple buttons. "There's no surveillance. It's also a no-fly zone. What is that place?"

"You have to be fucking kidding me," I said and rubbed my chin.

"What?" Aurelia asked.

"You don't think..." I sighed. "No, it's too crazy to even fathom."

Everyone in the room would laugh if I said what I'd been thinking. But the rumors about the place said it was some weird alien testing facility the humans had set up decades ago. Could it have been real all along and now they were using it to test on supernaturals?

"What are you thinking?" Ash asked.

"Nope, it's stupid. I want a tac team out there immediately. We need to see how good their security is, and best entry and exit points."

I turned on the news and sighed. Just like every other day, the camera showed supernaturals in magic-blocking cuffs being shuffled onto buses.

"I'm on it, boss," Dan said as he typed something on his phone.

"Even without the Council controlling them, this is still going on." Aurelia slumped in her seat.

"We don't know who else they had keeping them under control. I doubt Malcolm was strong enough to control all the humans."

"I have a team of five heading out in five minutes. The Fae warrior guy that the Princess brought back from Faery is going to transport them," Dan said, still staring at his phone.

"Good. The sooner we get some intel on this place, the better. I refuse to go in blind and risk everyone." I squeezed Aurelia's hand.

Her worry for Zeke flooded the bond, and I pulled her into my side. I was worried for the Rider as well. I'd thought along with the rest of them that he was dead. It was a relief to find out he was alive, but was it all an act? Was the human government trying to draw us out?

The news droned on in the background, like nothing else was going on in the world other than the "supernatural infestation", as they called it.

Other countries had followed the United States lead and began global witch trials, locking up anyone with a drop of supernatural blood.

"New developments in science today," the newscaster said brightly. "Scientists are one step closer to identifying and creating a blood test to check for supernatural heritage. This breakthrough will be a huge win for the war on supernaturals."

"They can do that?" Aurelia gasped.

"I would assume it's similar to those DNA kits that they have to check paternity."

That was not good for most supernaturals who had become adept at hiding in the shadows. If they made everyone take that blood test, even more supernaturals could be found and rounded up.

"We are well on our way to a national database for supernatural species. It's a huge victory and to be honest, I can't wait to take this test to prove that I'm human. It will be a relief to have that piece of paper to show everyone that I'm not a monster." The newscaster flipped her hair over her shoulder.

The man next to her put a finger to his ear and held up a hand. "We're getting word that the President is about to address the nation."

"I wonder what this is about?" I groaned.

"It can't be anything good." Ash straightened.

The camera flipped to the Rose Garden, where the President walked out to the podium, his expression grim. If this was about the new breakthrough, he wouldn't have looked like that. Dread pooled in my gut, but it wasn't all mine. Aurelia's feelings rushed down the bond as well.

"Hello, America, I have a heavy burden to bear today. Ten American soldiers have been declared missing in action. Yesterday they were sent to a supernatural stronghold to detain everyone in the building, but they were ambushed with magic. Some of the men who came back said they were knocked out and detained by these supernaturals." He paused to let that sink in.

"I had a feeling that was what this was about. Any word on a witch that can erase those humans' memories of where they have been?" I asked Dan.

"We don't have a witch here that can do it, and the ones from the outside I called didn't answer. I'm hoping they haven't been rounded up like the others." Dan hung his head.

"These are dangerous criminals. There is body cam footage of a shifter beheading a trusted ally of the American people. He will be sorely missed." He paused again.

"Not likely," I grumbled. "Did you check all the men in the cells for these body cams and listening devices?"

"Of course."

"The good news is that I have been informed that these supernaturals are the same as the ones who blew up the Dallas prison, and we have a powerful alliance that will eradicate them. We are also only weeks away from a federal mandate that will make testing for supernatural blood mandatory for every American."

The crowd around the President all started shouting questions at once. He held up a hand, but it didn't do a thing to stop them all from yelling. Mandatory testing was a controversial topic apparently.

"We have to do something. There's no space here, but we can't just leave people in those testing facilities." Aurelia clenched her hands into fists on the table.

"There has to be something we can do other than sit here and watch this vitriol," Ash grumbled.

He was itching to get Zeke back just as much as we were, probably more. They were Riders of the Hunt and had been brothers for millennia.

"There isn't much we can do but research the other facilities. You all don't have to be the ones who go into every single one of them to rescue people. I can send tactical teams," Dan said.

"No, we need to keep everyone we can here. We need them training and ready for war. I only sent one tac team out to scout that place for a reason," I said.

Fenrick peered closer at the computer screen. "We can still do the research for after the war. I don't think humans are going to stop persecuting supernaturals just because we win this war."

"I agree," Aurelia said.

She was still staring at the TV, where more and more lines of supernaturals were being herded like cattle onto buses. I wanted to turn the thing off but couldn't. We needed to keep tabs on what was happening in the world.

"Don't watch it, love. It's only upsetting you more." I rubbed her back in soothing circles.

"I can't just turn a blind eye to it. I have to watch it. If I don't see how the people are suffering, how can I hope to be a leader that will end that suffering for them?"

"But it's hurting you. I can feel through the bond how much." My chest ached with the pain she was feeling.

My mate was going to be an amazing queen because of her empathy.

"I'm sorry, I don't know how that works. I can't shut it off." She frowned.

"I don't want you to turn it off. I like knowing how you're feeling," I said.

"It's hurting you though." She glanced at me with watery eyes.

"Only because you're hurting, love. I'm strong. I can handle it."

"Um, Grey?" Fenrick frowned. "I think there's some truth to what the agent said."

"Why? What did you find?" I got up from the table and raced around to look at what he'd come across.

"I hacked into the database for one of the testing facilities we have yet to hit and found some videos of test subjects."

Aurelia rounded the table and was at my side in a second. "What is it?"

"Don't look, Princess. Some are pretty gruesome." Fenrick shuddered.

"I have to look. I have to know. I already told you all not to try to shield me from this." She crossed her arms.

Fenrick glanced up at me and I shrugged. I wasn't here to tell her what to do. As far as I was concerned, we were equals except when it came to her safety.

Fenrick turned back to the keyboard and typed a couple commands before a video played on the screen.

"This is test subject seventy-seven and we may just have a breakthrough today," the scientist on the screen said almost giddily.

The woman on the bed was blonde and had catlike features. She must have been some kind of cat shifter. Her eyes were closed but her face was contorted in pain as her body convulsed on the bed. The scientist turned to her, and a look of horror crossed his face as he screamed.

Foam bubbled from her mouth as the convulsions became even worse than before. She was dying. It resembled a human overdose. How much of that damn serum had they given that poor woman? Pain sliced through my chest as her hands shifted into black claws and then back. She was a jaguar shifter, and they were rare.

I wished I had known she was out in the world. I would have brought her to the Syndicate to train. That's why I had started the syndicate. I brought in rare supernaturals and gave them a purpose. She'd fallen through the cracks though.

The machines hooked to her flatlined and the scientist screamed as he grabbed some paddles to try to restart her heart. I hoped for the woman's sake that he was unsuccessful. She wouldn't suffer in the beyond.

"That poor woman," Aurelia whispered. "We have to stop this. They are killing supernaturals in the name of science."

"There's more," Fenrick said as he clicked another video.

"After the unfortunate incident yesterday," the scientist started speaking, "we are going to try something different today."

"Do I even want to know?" I asked.

"Probably not." Fenrick shuddered.

"This is test subject eighty-two. She is a known witch, and we are going to practice transference."

"What the hell? Is that what it sounds like? Are they trying to remove her magic?" I stared at Fenrick.

The brunette was tied to a table with tubes and electrodes all over her frail frame. The scientist flipped a switch, and the woman gasped as electricity flowed into her and Magic pooled at her fingertips. The giddy scientist brought over some kind of suction thing and attempted to suck the magic into a canister connected to it, but it wouldn't work.

"Release your power to me and the pain stops!" the scientist barked at the girl, but no matter how hard he tried, he couldn't suck away her magic.

"This is disgusting. I don't need to see any more to know we have to do something, but the question is, what?"

Chapter 19

AURELIA

"SIT DOWN, ASH." I glared at him, but my face softened when I saw the worry in his eyes.

We'd all seen the horrific videos of the testing facility. I shuddered as I remembered the witch dying on the table as the scientist lost his temper and turned up the voltage. They weren't people to him, they were just test subjects. It was disgusting, and I prayed to whatever gods were listening that Zeke could survive it until we were able to get him out of there.

"I can't!" Ash bellowed. "Where is the tactical team? It's been two days of silence. We need to go in."

"We don't have any information on the place, Ash. We could be walking to our deaths if we try without any kind of recon." I reminded him for probably the hundredth time.

I glanced back down at the book in front of me. It was the golden book I'd been searching for this whole time, but so far it hadn't given me any insight into how to defeat the Council. Had I been wrong all along? Was the book not important? Was I banking all my hopes on a book that didn't actually have a way to stop them?

I had been going through the book for days but nothing in it had called to me. We'd risked our lives for that book. There had to be a reason. There had to be something.

"Where's Magna?" I asked Dan.

She's helping with rations today. Why?" he asked.

"I need to speak to her about this useless book." I pointed to the gold book with a huff of frustration.

Why had she thought this was the key? Why had I thought the same before I poured my own memories into the other book?

"I'm sure it's not useless if Magna sent you to find it knowing she would end up in prison and tortured after, Princess." Dan raised an eyebrow.

I slumped back in my chair. He had a point. Magna was a powerful seer, so she would have known what would happen when we went to get the book, but the sneaky woman never told us all the facts. It could mess up the future. She'd told us *that* all the time.

The news played in the background as I continued flipping pages. They were all excited that a breakthrough had been made in identifying supernatural DNA. It was a lot more complex than human DNA and had taken scientists a while to figure it out, but now they had it narrowed down, and they were working on a test.

The lengths they would go to so they could eradicate us from existence were terrifying. We would be gone soon if I couldn't find a way to defeat the damn Council. I glanced back at the book and continued flipping through the pages.

"Magna will be here soon. Don't be harsh with her. She has a heavy burden to bear. She also went through hell in that prison." Dan sat next to me at the table.

"I would never be harsh with her. Magna is my friend even if she is cryptic half the time." I flipped another page but I was barely paying attention.

"You asked to see me, Princess?" Magna said as she glided into the room.

"What's with the *Princess* shit? You never call me that." I crossed my arms over my chest.

"I figured I should get used to calling you by your title." She grinned and sat down on my other side.

"You're just screwing with me. You knew I was going to get frustrated and ask to see you today, didn't you?"

"Of course, I did. I know all, remember?" She chuckled.

"You don't know all." I shook my head.

How could she be so light when everything seemed so bleak? I was drowning in misery and responsibility. There were so many things I needed to do. I needed to free the supernaturals from the testing facilities, and defeat the Council, but I had no idea how I was going to do any of those things.

"There's nothing here." I stabbed my finger into the page of the book. "I've gone through it a hundred times, and I'm still not finding anything that can stop the Council."

"Are you sure? Maybe you're not looking for the right thing." She raised a brow.

"You're telling me what? I need to put my intentions into scanning the pages?" I scoffed.

"No, but maybe it's the spells you're looking for that are the problem."

"I'm looking for something that can defeat the Council." I threw my hands up.

"If you're looking for a death spell, then you definitely won't find what you're looking for in that book." Magna tapped the golden pages.

"How else am I supposed to defeat the Council then?" I asked.

They wouldn't stop coming after us all until they were eradicated. How could I possibly win the war and not kill them? That didn't make sense.

"When one army defeats another, is that other army always all killed?" she asked in her usual riddles.

"No, the survivors are usually spared, but the Council must atone for their crimes. You didn't see the videos of the experiments they had human scientists performing." I shuddered.

"Yes, they need to pay, but why does a book of light magic need to be the answer? How do you stop them and then try them for their crimes? Isn't that the question you should be asking yourself, Princess?" Magna grinned.

I sat back in my seat and glanced over at Dan, who was typing away at his phone, pretending he wasn't listening, but I knew he was.

"So, I can't kill them in battle, or I would be unjust?" I asked, and Magna nodded.

How was that just? I'd watched videos of supernaturals dying because of the experiments they were performing on them. How many had they murdered in their quest for ultimate power?

"I can see the wheels spinning in your head, Princess," Dan said, never glancing up from his phone. "You will be a just ruler, but I think what Magna is saying is that if those assholes die quickly in battle, the people won't get the closure they need. That's why it would be unjust."

"When did you become a philosopher? It had to have happened after you shot me with a sedative dart and put all this into motion," I snarked back at him.

Dan grinned at me. We'd become allies since that had happened. I didn't exactly know when we had, but he was a good person, and I knew he'd just been following orders. No one could have predicted that would start this whole mess we found ourselves in.

"You're still going on about that?" He laughed. "I thought we'd moved past that, Princess."

"Never." I bumped his shoulder with mine and turned back to Magna. "So, this book will give me the answers I need to defeat the Council as long as my goal isn't their death in battle?"

"Correct," Magna said and stood.

"Where are you going?" I asked as she walked back to the door.

"Grey will be here soon with news, and I am still needed elsewhere. You know what you're looking for now, Princess. You don't need my help."

I slumped back in my chair, unsure if I really knew what I needed. The way to defeat them wasn't death. It couldn't be. I glanced back down at the book, and something on the open page snagged my attention. I leaned in closer. It was a binding spell.

"Did you find something?" Dan asked with a grin.

"That crazy Fae led me to the exact spot I needed without me even noticing," I grumbled.

"You expected anything less from her? She may speak in riddles, but she always leads you to exactly where you need to be, precisely when you need to be there." Dan laughed.

I ignored him mostly because I didn't want to tell him he was right. I scoured the pages reading the binding spell. It could bind the Council's powers forever and make them basically human. It wasn't until I got to the last page of the spell that I noticed there was a warning.

This spell should only be used in the most dire of circumstances, and only by a powerful, Royal Fae. If the gods don't deem the caster worthy of binding, all will be lost. Binding Fae is almost as gruesome as death. They will be human without their magic. Heed this warning, because the penalty is death if the gods don't approve.

Chills raced down my spine at the words. I was a powerful Royal Fae, probably the most powerful in the realm, and the Council deserved a lot more than becoming human. The warning still chilled me to the bone, though. What if the gods didn't deem me worthy of performing the spell? What if they decided I wasn't worthy of the throne? Would using this spell kill me?

I chewed my lip nervously as Ash continued to pace. I stared at him as he walked back and forth across the room with glassy, unfocused eyes. He hadn't paid any attention to the conversation we'd just had so he wouldn't know that the spell I'd just found was dangerous.

I decided then and there that I couldn't tell anyone about the warning in the book. I had to keep it to myself, or they would stop me from using it.

"What did you find?" Dan asked with a raised brow.

"Something that could turn the tide in this war with the Council, but if I told you, I would have to kill you." I closed the book so no one could see the page I was on.

It was written in Fae, and even though Dan was only half, he'd never been taught to read Fae. My secret was safe from him, but I didn't want my father or Fenrick seeing the page it had been open to. They would tell Grey in a heartbeat, and all would be lost.

Just as Magna had said, Grey came rushing into the office a moment later, his eyes wide with worry and anger.

"What is it?" I jumped from the chair and rushed to his side.

The expression on his face was grim as he glanced between the three of us. "The scouts are back, and the news isn't good at all."

What do you mean? What happened?" I asked and wrung my hands together.

Please don't tell me they're all dead. Please don't tell me we're too late to save Zeke. It was my fault he was taken. If I had fought harder against Grey and Ash, we would have seen he wasn't dead. We could have dragged him out of that gala. He never would have been in that place at all.

"The place was fortified and guarded to the extreme. The scouts barely made it out with their lives," Grey said as he wrapped his arms around me.

"Did they get inside?" Ash asked.

"No, it was exactly as I'd thought. The humans have been using that base for years, but everyone thought it was an urban legend."

"What are you talking about?" I asked with a frown.

"The place they took the supernaturals that only a few people know about is also the site where it was rumored they were testing on aliens. It's top-secret and a no-fly zone. No one ever thought it really existed, but we know it does now because the high profile supernaturals are being taken to Area 51."

"You have to be joking," I said.

How the hell were we supposed to get into Area 51? It was the highest security military base in the entire world. It was an urban legend, right?

Hopelessness tore through me. Human technology was too advanced for us to just walk in and rescue people. We were totally fucked.

Chapter 20

GREY

I GRABBED Aurelia's hand and we rushed to the elevator. I hadn't seen the tactical team yet. I was too worried about telling my mate the news.

We couldn't get Zeke out. Not yet, anyway.

My mate's hopelessness flooded the bond. She knew as well as I did, we couldn't go busting into fucking Area 51 and get people out. It wasn't possible, even for supernaturals.

"Let's talk to the scouts and then we'll see if we can come up with a plan." I rubbed her shoulder.

"Okay," she said softly.

The elevator doors opened to the infirmary, and I scanned the beds. "I thought you sent a team of six."

"Shit. Where are the others?" Dan cursed.

"This is all that made it back?" Aurelia asked, covering her lips with her fingers.

She walked over to the bed nearest us, and I recognized the Fae warrior she'd brought back from the castle. He was beaten and bloody, barely conscious.

"Ambush," he said.

"It was a trap. The agent lied to us." I clenched my hand into a fist.

Anger pulsed through me, and I wanted to go down to the cells and beat him bloody. The warrior pushed himself to sit.

"I don't know if he lied or if they were just ready for any possibility. We were scouting the area for an entire day before we were ambushed by the military. There are definitely people being taken there, though."

"Did you get close enough to see any entry or exit points?" I asked.

Even though we weren't going to be able to go in and get them now, that didn't mean all the information we could gather wouldn't be useful.

"No, they must have some high-tech sensors or something, because the second we were past a certain point, we were ambushed." He shook his head.

Fenrick crossed the room to us and held out his hands, but the warrior shook him off. "I'm Fae. I'll heal."

Aurelia cocked a brow at him. "Don't be stubborn. Let Fenrick help speed up the healing process."

"Yes, Your Highness." He smirked.

"Smart ass. You look half dead and you're still acting like a smart ass." She rolled her eyes.

"You saw them bringing people in?" I asked, getting us back on track.

"I did. The same buses that have been all over the news were coming and going that first day."

Dan stepped up next to me. "Where is the rest of the team?"

"Either dead or captured. I tried to get us all out of there but they closed ranks on us and split us up so I couldn't get a handle on everyone. I thought Duke was the one with the worst injuries, but I was stabbed in the gut right before I sifted us out."

Four more casualties in a war we never wanted to fight. If they were in the testing facility there, we were definitely going to have to get in and free our people. I just didn't know how.

"Is there a chance they're still fighting or were left out there to die?" Dan ran a hand down his face.

"I tried to go back but before I could, the scouts at the wards brought me in. I don't think I could have done much anyway. I passed out the second we got inside."

"No, you did good," I said, clapping him on the shoulder.

"We need to speed up the timeline on this war." Aurelia sat in the chair next to the bed. "Maybe if we establish the new rule of law in Faery, we can reason with the humans, and they will let our people go home to Faery."

"You think that's possible?" Dan asked. "Right now, the Council is controlling the testing, and I'm sure they're controlling what the humans have access to."

"If we take them out, the humans will have free rein to test on anyone in their custody." I gripped Aurelia's chair.

"I want to think that they could be reasoned with. We don't want to go to war with the humans, but they can't detain our people like this either." Aurelia glanced up into my eyes.

"We'll figure that out when it comes to it, love." I patted her shoulder and leaned down to kiss her forehead.

"I think I found a way for me to defeat the Council," she whispered.

Her unease pulsed through the bond. She didn't want to tell me what she'd found. What was it that had her so freaked out?

"How?" Dan asked.

"The golden book." She shook her head at him. "You were there when Magna told me I was looking at this all wrong."

"Yes, Princess, but you didn't tell me how." He crossed his arms.

"It's complicated, but I need to get close to them." She chewed her lip.

There was something she wasn't telling us.

"It's too dangerous going anywhere near the Council," I said.

"Grey, you know I have to do this." She stood from her chair and faced me.

"No. Whatever this is will be too dangerous. We just need to take them out and be done with it."

Dan was shaking his head before I finished my sentence. "Magna said that won't work."

"That's how I was looking at everything—all wrong." Aurelia pointed at Dan. "The book doesn't kill. It's a book of light."

"How do we defeat them without killing them?" My knuckles turned white, I was gripping the chair so hard.

"They need to be tried in front of the people. If we don't, we ruin our relationship with them. I will be seen as unjust if I set out to kill them."

"This is war, Aurelia. People die in war," I said.

She hung her head, not meeting my eyes. She knew how dangerous this plan was. Was she expecting she wouldn't survive?

"I understand that more than you know, Grey."

"We're not discussing this anymore. We will figure out another plan that keeps you safe," I growled.

"Oh, we're not discussing this, huh? And I don't get a say in it? We're bonded, but that doesn't mean you get to make decisions for me." Her face turned red, and anger flared through the bond.

Shit. I'd really stepped in it. I sent my regret down the bond to her, but she wasn't having it. She glared at me in return.

"Aurelia, we have to do this my way. I can't lose you." I hung my head.

"You're not hearing me. You're letting your stubbornness rule your damn brain. We can't kill the Council." She threw her hands up in the air.

"I don't care what Magna said, or what the people of the realm think!" I roared. "I care about your safety."

Dan planted his hands on his hips. "Killing the Council is the safest option. You are the princess of the realm and meant to rule. We have to think about your safety, Princess."

"You too?" she scoffed, rounding on Dan.

"You shouldn't even be fighting in the war." He said the wrong thing, and I flinched in sympathy.

Aurelia poked him in his chest and then clenched her hand into a fist. She pulled her arm back to punch the idiot, but Fenrick grabbed her arm and pulled her back behind him.

"Our royalty have been warriors throughout the centuries. Aurelia is no different. She has proven time and again that she is capable, yet you all still doubt her? Shame on all of you."

"Thank you, Fenrick." Aurelia glared at me and Dan in turn.

"I'm not done yet, Princess." Fenrick raised a brow at her. "At the same time, you need to remember that their worry comes from a place of love and respect. Everyone wants to return to Faery, but they want to go home to the place they remember. You are the only one who can give them that and as such, must be protected."

Aurelia instantly deflated. "Fine. We need a compromise then."

"You're going to put that plan into action whether I like it or not, aren't you?" I asked.

My stubborn mate wasn't about to back down, but what if I could convince her to have guards while she did it? The Riders of the Hunt loved her like a sister. I'd bet they would take up positions around her and protect her while she got close to the Council to enact her plan.

A commotion in the hall grabbed my attention, and I spun to the door to the infirmary. Fenrick and Dan moved almost as fast as I did to block the possible threat to Aurelia.

She rolled her eyes as a shifter burst through the door with heaving breaths. She slapped their backs and they both moved so she could walk to him. He was a scout trusted to watch the wards, and no threat to her. I sighed with relief as I waited for him to catch his breath. Had he run up the stairs to get to the infirmary?

"You have something to report?" Dan asked.

"Yes… sir," he wheezed.

"Give him a second to catch his breath." I shook my head at Dan.

"If it's so important that he ran all the way here, we may not have time for that," Dan said.

"Council," he said breathily.

"The Council? What about them?" Aurelia asked, her eyes wide.

"Here," he answered.

"Are you telling me the Council is inside the building?" I growled.

"No… wards."

"Shit. They found us?" I asked.

The man nodded, and I grabbed the remote for the TVs and switched it to the surveillance footage from outside the building. They were bringing their attack to us. Half the people in that room were on the Council's most wanted list and we were out of time.

"How did they find us?" Dan asked but didn't appear to expect an answer.

"We're you followed?" I asked the warrior still in the bed.

"It's possible. I have heard that the Council has the power to follow the signature when sifting, but I thought it was just a rumor."

"It's not," Fenrick confirmed. "But the person has to be in close proximity during the sift to follow it, so there were Fae there when you sifted out, and they alerted the Council to our location."

"Fuck," the warrior said, hanging his head.

"It's not your fault. You couldn't have known," Aurelia said with determination. "We wanted to move up the timeline so we could get our people out of the testing facilities. This just gave us what we already wanted."

I glanced at my mate warily. Her determined glare ate away at something inside me. She wasn't going to listen to reason, and that announcement had gotten us out of our argument without a solution.

I glared at the TV. The Council had their entire army at our wards, using magic to try to get past them. They couldn't, which gave me a small bit of relief. Aurelia was stronger than them, but she wasn't as experienced.

"We need to sound the alarm. War has come for us," I said.

Aurelia turned to the scout with a frown. "Get all civilians to a safe place, now. Everyone else needs to get to the garage."

The man glanced at Dan, who nodded to do as she said. Aurelia growled low in her throat. Dan caught on to her displeasure and glared at the scout.

"Do not defer to me when the princess of our realm gives you an order. She outranks me."

A deafening boom rocked the ward, and I stumbled. It seemed if they couldn't get in subtly, they were going to use brute force. Fuck. War was inevitable, and it was happening now.

Chapter 21

AURELIA

RAGE POURED THROUGH ME, but I couldn't act on it. We needed to get our army together. As soon as the elevator doors opened, I was racing to the garage and scanning faces for my father. He needed to find the warriors we freed from mind control while Fenrick went to our rebel army.

"Fenrick, follow me." I waved a hand at him.

Fenrick kept pace with me as I searched for my father. He had to be there with everyone. He was a warrior king. Like Fenrick had said, we came from a long line of warriors. I finally spotted him in the back corner where weapons were being handed out to the army.

I waved a hand to get his attention, and he made his way to Fenrick and me. He raised a brow at me as I waited for him.

"I need you to go to the house in the dark forest and alert the warriors we freed that war is starting," I said.

My father grinned. "Why don't you go alert your army, and I'll fight the Council in your place?"

I bristled at his thinly veiled attempt to keep me out of battle. All these overprotective males were going to turn me prematurely gray.

"Nice try, Dad, but we all know I have to be the one to fight the Council." I squared my shoulders.

"It was worth a shot." He kissed my forehead. "Don't put yourself at unnecessary risk."

"Any risk I take will be calculated and absolutely necessary. I can promise you that." I hugged him hard.

My father gasped like I'd shocked him and when he pulled away, tears shined in his eyes. "I'm so proud of you, daughter. Give them hell."

I didn't know if I would ever see him again. The binding spell was complicated and could end in my death, but at least the Council would no longer have their magic and my parents could try them for their crimes, and usher in their own new era without me if that's what the Fates decided.

"I will," I said with tears streaking down my face.

I wiped them away and turned to Fenrick. He was the friend I'd tormented as a child. The one person I could play hide and seek with, even though he hated it. He'd never figured out how I always hid so well from him. I smiled softly.

"Don't do that, Your Highness. You're not sacrificing yourself. Promise me." Fenrick choked on his words.

"I'm not sacrificing myself, I'm doing everything I must to take them down." I rolled my shoulders back.

"Why do you look like you don't expect to see me again then?" He gripped both my biceps in his hands.

"This is war, Fenrick. There are always going to be casualties in war." I sighed.

"If I come back with the rebels and find you took unnecessary risks to protect the realms, I will be so angry with you, Princess," he choked out.

"I'm not doing that. We need the rebels here. Now. I don't have much of an army here without them. Please don't make this harder than it already is." I deflated.

I didn't want to disappoint anyone, but with the binding spell, I didn't even know if I would survive this. These goodbyes weren't what I would have wanted them to be, but I needed to make sure that they knew that I wasn't being reckless, I was making sure they all lived.

That they would be free of the Council's atrocities, and able to remove our people from the human detention centers. We needed to save our people and when I said we, I knew in my bones it would come down to me. I'd always known it.

"I'm going to the rebels now. Be careful, Your Highness." Fenrick bowed his head and sifted from the garage.

Why was he suddenly being so formal? What was I missing?

Strong arms wrapped around my waist from behind, and I stiffened. My anger bubbled to the surface, and I attempted to break the hold.

"My love, I'm sorry." He spun me around in his arms.

I glared at him as he leaned down, taking my breath away in a hard kiss. I gripped his shirt in an attempt to push him away, but my hands didn't get the memo as I just pulled him closer. When he deepened the kiss, it was like our souls connected on some primal level. Grey growled into the kiss, the vibrations pouring through me.

"I just need you safe, love," he said after we broke apart.

The army was all around us. We didn't have time for another argument.

"Grey, we always knew from the beginning that this was going to come down to me, and the fact that you don't think I can do it hurts beyond belief." I shook my head.

"What? It's not about your capabilities, my love. It's the fact that we just bonded, and we're supposed to spend eternity together. I want a good deal of that time spent on this side of the veil. I want little princes and princesses we can spoil rotten. I want a life with you."

Tears streaked in rivers down my face at his words because that was what I wanted too, but it was up to Fate now. I had to do this. I had to defeat the Council and try them for their crimes. The only way to do that was with the binding spell.

"No, love, don't cry." He leaned his forehead against mine.

"If the gods deem it so, then that's what we'll have. It's everything I want for our lives, but the realm needs to be safe first, and the only way to make it safe is to win this war and defeat the Council my way." I stared directly into his eyes, hoping he would listen finally.

"Fine, but not alone," Grey said. "I will be leading the army, and you will hang back until you can get a look at the Council and do your thing."

"I just sent my father and Fenrick to get our allies in Faery. They can surround the Council guards and we can win this fight faster than we thought possible."

Especially if my plan works.

It had to work. The book wouldn't have opened to that page randomly without it being the only way. Magna had said I needed an option that wouldn't kill.

I stepped out of the garage and into the bright sunlight. It shouldn't have been a beautiful sunny day when this battle took place. Were the gods laughing at us as we fought for our own survival? Is that why it was a perfect, warm day when blood would be shed in this place?

The army all stared at me with trepidation. Most of them worked at the Syndicate and knew how to hold their own, but many were those we'd rescued from regular lives among the humans.

They weren't trained, but they wanted to help and had been working hard to make a difference. I was proud of them. We were still far enough away from the wards that Ronaldo and his army of assholes wouldn't see us as I faced the crowd.

I held up a hand, and the chattering stopped as all eyes were on me. "I was an orphan, or at least I thought I was. Even at the age of nine, I was working toward this day. The day we would take down the corrupt Council who wants to see us as slaves."

The crowd roared, and a figure among them stared back at me. What the hell was Magna doing with the warriors? She shouldn't be fighting. A sprite zipped by her side, and I gasped. My little pixie friend couldn't be heard over the crowd, but I could guess she was cursing the Council and calling for their deaths for her sister. I smiled at them and nodded.

I held my hand up to calm the crowd. "We are about to go into battle. We aren't going into this for the same reasons the Council is, though. We aren't at war for the same reasons the humans have warred for centuries. We go to war now for our very survival." I sighed.

Grey stepped forward. "The Council wants to control us and if they can't control us, they want us all dead. I've seen the videos of the experiments they have been performing. If we don't defeat them now, we may never stop them."

Grey wrapped an arm around my waist, and another cheer went up from the large group. They liked the fact that we were a united front, even though I wasn't quite sure how long that would last.

"King and Queen, King and Queen, King and Queen," the crowd chanted, and I gasped.

I wasn't the queen, even though Grey was technically the Shifter King already, but I couldn't be the Shifter Queen. I wasn't a shifter.

"The army is letting us know who they're fighting for, love." Grey kissed my temple, and the crowd roared louder.

"I'm not a queen, Grey," I whispered as I stared out over the crowd.

"You're a princess and married to the Shifter King. You may as well be queen." He raised a hand to silence the masses.

"The Council is trying to destroy everything, including our way of life. We won't let them take that from us, will we?" Grey roared.

People were stomping and screaming, and I was sure we could be heard all the way back in Dallas city limits, they were going so crazy.

Grey and me together obviously gave our army hope. I just prayed they would still have that hope after I did what I had to.

Dan stepped up beside me and handed me my bag. I glanced inside and found the gold book. He winked at me, then nodded and squeezed my shoulder.

That was all the affirmation I was going to get from him. Even though he'd voiced his concerns earlier, he was behind me and that warmed my heart.

"Are we ready to win this war?" Dan roared.

The warriors went insane, banging on anything they could find, still stomping their feet. "Get into position and let's show the greedy Fae Council who's boss."

With that, the warriors dispersed to get into position, and Grey spun me around once more. He kissed me hard, and his arms wrapped around my waist. It felt like a goodbye, and tears streamed down my cheeks. This couldn't be goodbye. It wouldn't be.

Why did the Fates have to be so cruel? I couldn't have even a year with my mate before everything went to hell?

"Grey, I love you. No matter what. Please remember that no matter what happens." I kissed him softly.

"You're making me want to put you in the cell with Lydia until this blows over, love." He leaned his forehead against mine.

"I think that might be worse than facing the Council." I frowned.

"Whatever you do, love, don't die. Promise me."

"I can't promise you that any more than you can promise me, but I will do everything in my power to come back to you. In this life and in any other. That I can promise, my love." I called him my love like he so often did to me because that was exactly what he was.

Grey was the love of my life, and even if I did go to the beyond that day, I would always come back to him.

We would be together for eternity, even if taking out the Council killed me. I would make sure of it.

Chapter 22

GREY

AS I PULLED AWAY from Aurelia, her words didn't sit well with me. Was she planning on dying in this ward? That was completely unacceptable. She had to survive. She would usher in a new era, which was what the prophecy had said.

Now that I was thinking about the prophecy, I cursed myself in my head. It said she would usher in a new era for supernaturals, but it never said she would live to see that era. Was she meant to die? I couldn't bear the thought.

She'd promised not to take unnecessary risks, but what was the spell she'd found in the book?

I turned her in my arms and cupped her cheeks. "I need you to promise me you'll stay back a safe distance to complete the spell on the Council. I need to know you're at least somewhat safe."

"I will stay back as far as I can to complete the spell," she said and nodded. "I have to do this, Grey. I must complete this spell."

"I know, love. Just be safe and come back to me," I said and spotted Magna.

I wanted to have a conversation with the seer before we went to war.

I tore myself away from my mate, and beelined to Magna.

"What is she about to do?" I asked.

"I don't know what you're talking about, Grey," she said too casually.

"Yes, you do. What is she planning? You told her that we couldn't kill the Council in this war, and I want to know what you showed her," I growled.

"The Book of Light doesn't have death spells. She was searching in earnest for something that wasn't the correct answer. I pointed her in the right direction."

"Does the right direction end in her death?" I asked, crossing my arms.

If Magna said yes, then I didn't know what I was going to do. We'd been allies for centuries on Earth, but if she lost me my mate, I would never forgive her.

"Every decision that immortals make shows me a different timeline, Grey. You know this. We have discussed it many times. I cannot be sure if this time the decision to use the spell will end in her death, but the depth of your love her for her, and the love of those closest to her, makes it highly improbable."

"That's not good enough for me."

"I knew you were going to say that, Grey. We have had this same conversation in my head a hundred times." Magna smirked. "You need to trust in your mate and your family. That's the way to make sure you both survive this battle."

"Family?" I scoffed. "I have no family, Magna, and you know it."

"You don't?" she asked, hurt lacing her tone. "So the found family that you have been working with for centuries doesn't count?"

"That's not what I meant, and you know it, Mags. I'm sorry. I'm just lost and confused. I need direct answers, not riddles." I sighed.

"It's not riddles. Trust your gut and the people closest to you. They won't let you down. They would rather die than see the princess fall. Trust us."

Ash and the other Riders were huddled in the corner, watching Aurelia like they knew something was up. I nodded to Magna.

"I trust you all with my life, but I would give that up for her to live."

"Trust that we all know that and would do the same. I wouldn't have helped her if it wasn't the only way." Magna lowered her head.

"How many futures have you seen, and how many does she die in?" I asked.

"I have seen infinite futures and some more terrible than others, but out of those where she enacts this plan, there's more that end with her alive than her death, Grey. Trust your people and trust yourself." She nodded and then walked away.

What the fuck was I supposed to do with that? There were more riddles than truth. Magna hadn't told me exactly what the plan was, but the odds were higher this way that my mate would live. Only if the right decisions were made, though.

I stalked toward the Riders. They were a somber bunch now that Zeke was possibly locked in a bunker in Nevada. I stared at Asher, and he broke off from the group of his brothers.

"You love Aurelia like a sister," I said.

"Is that even a question?" Asher asked.

"No, it was a statement. She agreed to hang back and take down the Council. I need to be at the front line to lead our troops. I need someone to protect her. I don't know exactly what she's planning, but I know there's a chance she won't survive it."

"How do you know that?" Ash asked.

His tone was angry, like the thought of Aurelia not surviving this battle made him murderous. I felt the same. She had to survive, and if I couldn't be there to make sure of it, there was no one else I wanted at her back to ensure her safety.

"Magna said there is a chance that she might not survive, but free will and decisions made always have a hand in Fate. She said to trust myself and trust my family, so I'm trusting in my brothers. The Riders of the Hunt will protect her even from herself."

"You have my word as a Rider that I will do everything in my power to keep the princess safe, Grey. I would have done it even if you hadn't asked. She is our hope for a new world." Ash shook his head and held out his hand.

I took his hand in mine and nodded. Relief flooded me. I trusted Ash with her life. He'd protected Aurelia on numerous occasions, even from me when that was what she needed. He would watch out for her, and my focus wouldn't be divided in this battle. We would come out victorious even if the Council thought they had us cornered.

War was bloody, and we would have casualties, but in the end, the Council would fall. I would make sure of it.

I raced out of the garage to the front lines of our warriors. They were beating swords against shields, and many had already shifted into their animals. My gaze followed Ash and his brothers as they made their way to Aurelia and circled around her.

Aurelia's irritation flared through the bond as she said something to him that I couldn't hear at that distance. Ash shrugged and pointed in my direction. *Fucking traitor.*

He was selling me out to my mate, but I didn't have time to think about that as Ronaldo's high-pitched squeak of a laugh grated on my ears.

"You think you can defeat my army that has been fighting for centuries with that group?" Ronaldo laughed again.

"We have something they don't!" I roared to my warriors.

"And what is that?" Ronaldo asked mockingly.

"We are fighting for our right to live. We're fighting for our families and for our children, so they aren't oppressed or sent to testing facilities to be lab rats and casualties in the Council's quest for ultimate power over all the realms. They are fighting for greed, but us? We are fighting for our lives, and that makes us far more dangerous!" I screamed.

The crowd in front of me roared, and I could even spot Aurelia's whoop in the back of the throng. She had Riders of the Hunt surrounding her, and her irritation flooded the bond at that fact, but she was also inspired by my speech.

"For life!" I bellowed as I turned and raced for the wards with my army at my back.

How long would it be before Fenrick and the king were back with reinforcements? We needed them surrounded to win this thing, and I'd hoped that mine and Aurelia's speeches would have given me enough time.

The Council hadn't been able to get through our wards, so all they could do was wait until our ranks crashed through them, into their soldiers. I wondered where Aurelia was as I cut down a Council guard.

"If you can, avoid the ones with blank expressions," I said at the last second.

They would still come after us, but if we could detain them instead of kill them, it would beneficial for everyone in the future.

I pulled my sword from my sheath, but several shifted warriors stepped in front of me and took out the guards with teeth and claws. I recognized them as shifters from the prison. They had as much of a vendetta against the Council as I did. They hadn't been experimented on, but the only reason they weren't was because of my mate.

They were loyal, but I was fighting this battle too. I didn't need to be protected. I flinched at the thought. Aurelia had said something similar, and now I was getting angry that I was being protected.

I was the Shifter King. I needed to realize people would try to protect me above all else. Just like I expected my mate to understand. Shit. I'd been an ass. How could I expect people not to protect me but get mad when she felt the same?

I sent apologies down the bond to her, but nothing came back. Terror flooded me as I couldn't get a read on my mate's emotions.

What was she doing that she wasn't pouring her feelings down the bond? She didn't know how to shut them off. I roared out a battle cry, and my sword sliced through a Council guard. His eyes were clear. He agreed with their greed.

Did he think they would be on the winning side? If so, he was sorely mistaken. My army had nothing else. If the Council won, we would be eradicated. This was our final stand, and we would make sure it counted.

My sword clanged against a guard with blank eyes, and I spun around him and hit him in the back of the head with the hilt of my dagger. He wasn't there of his own free will. He was just as much of a victim as the rest of us. I wished I had Aurelia's power to release them from the mind control.

My fingers tingled along with my spine as I had the thought. Was it possible I had that power too? I didn't even know how magic worked, or what happened when a Fae mated with a shifter. It rarely happened.

I brought a hand up and the next blank-eyed warrior I came across, I let the magic fly. It hit him on the forehead, and he crumpled to the ground with a groan.

"What happened?" The man blinked up at me.

"Whose side are you on?" I asked as I pointed my sword at his throat.

"What do you mean? Are you at war with the Shadow King?" The man was confused.

"You were fighting with the Council a second ago against the Shadow Kingdom and the rest of the supernaturals," I growled. "So whose side are you on?"

The man's eyes widened, and he shook his head. "My allegiance is to the Shadow Kingdom. I told the Council to go fuck themselves."

"Good," I said and helped the man up.

He pushed me out of the way just in time to block another sword at my back. Fuck, that had been close. I grinned at the man before we stood back-to-back. There were both clear-eyed guards and mind-controlled guards circling us.

"Did you get me out of whatever they did to me?" the guy asked in awe.

"I did," I said.

"Do it for them. We can turn the tide." He pointed to the others around us.

"I don't know if I can do it again," I admitted. "I wasn't even sure I did it to you when I fixed you."

"You need to try, or we're all screwed, and even more people will die," he said, and I had to admit he was right, but how could I do it?

Would I be dooming our entire army, or was Aurelia going to help us get out of this yet again?

"I'll do what I can, but I can't make any promises."

Chapter 23

AURELIA

"WHERE ARE YOU GOING, PRINCESS?" Ash grabbed my biceps and pulled me back.

"I'm going to find the Council." I ripped my arm from the Rider's grasp.

"You're going to find the Council. Princess, you realize what a bad idea that is, right?" he asked.

"I have to end this before too many people die." I turned to leave, but Asher's brothers were all blocking me.

"You're going to get close to the Council and do what? I was asked not to leave your side, and I need to know what we're getting into here." Ash crossed his arms.

I gripped the book in my hand as I scanned the battlefield for a place I could start the spell. "I don't need to be super close to them, but close enough that I can see them and perform the spell."

"Fine, but I want you out of the way of the fighting. We'll protect you, even if we have to protect you from yourself."

"Thank you." I flipped the book open to the page I needed as I ran behind the Riders of the Hunt.

One by one they broke off from the group as Council guards attacked them with their swords. I glanced up at the clanging of metal and into the blank eyes of a Council guard. I knew I shouldn't do it because the spell was already going to take almost everything I had, but my magic swirled inside me, needing to rid the man of the mind control he was under.

I flung my magic at him and hit him in the face. He crumpled to the ground at Ash's feet and groaned. He blinked up at me from the ground, and his eyes widened.

"The Council controlled your mind. We're at war. Go!" I shouted.

The soldier scrambled to his feet and sprinted toward the Council guards. I sprinted to a quiet spot, and the trees moved to give me cover as I read from the book.

"Princess, you can't use that spell." Ash reached for the book in my hand, but I dodged him.

"You can read that?" I asked in shock.

"Yes, and that spell is too dangerous, even for someone as powerful as you. It's meant to be a last resort. It's meant to require everything the caster has."

"I know that. This is our last resort, Ash, don't you see that? We don't have any other options. I scoured this book for something to help us, and this is the only way." I shook my head.

Ash deflated. I had him. He knew this was what I had to do. The battle raged around us, and more Council guards poured into our forest by the second. I couldn't use my power on the ones that were being controlled. I just needed to bide my time until the spell was complete.

A battle cry filled the space, and I glanced up. Fenrick and Santori were there. They charged the enemy from the back of their ranks with a roar. Our reinforcements had arrived. Thank the gods they'd arrived in time.

Our people from the Syndicate were good, but they'd been outnumbered at least two to one. The battle raged on, supernaturals fighting against each other for the very right to live in peace. I hated that it had come to this. War was always messy.

"You're not going to let me talk you out of this, are you? Does

Grey know?" Ash placed a hand on my shoulder as he leaned down to read more of the spell.

"He knows I have something that will stop the Council, but he doesn't know what it is. We fought over it earlier." I glanced away.

I scanned the battlefield for any glimpse of Grey, but he was in the thick of the fight. I couldn't see him anywhere. I sent up a prayer to the gods that he would be okay and live up to the title of Shifter King for a long time to come before I turned back to Ash.

"I'm doing this. If I don't, then all is lost, and the Council continues their tyranny."

Ash snapped the book closed in my hands. "Not if I take this from you, Princess. You didn't tell Grey what a dangerous spell this was."

"I don't have to run everything past him because he's my mate. We have all known from the beginning that defeating them was going to fall completely on my shoulders. Well, it has, and I must do this."

A scream tore through the battlefield that could be heard over the clanging of metal. I turned to see a shifter in their tiger form tearing through an enemy soldier. There was so much blood and death. I was the only one who could stop the carnage.

I had to do something. I had to say something to convince Ash to let me do this. His hands still trapped mine around the book. He wasn't letting go, no matter how hard I tugged on it.

"Don't make me waste my magic on you, Ash. I must do this. We both know my magic might not be enough. This has to work," I said, glaring at the Rider.

Ash sighed and hung his head, but he finally released the book and stepped away. "You better survive this, Princess. They call us Riders of the Hunt for a reason. We can ride anywhere, and we will ride straight across the veil and drag you back if we have to."

I took a huge breath and opened the book. The pages fluttered instantly to the one I needed.

A loud voice boomed over the sounds of the battle, "We can stop this right now, just hand over the princess."

Ronaldo thought he could bargain with us? It wouldn't change the outcome. If they handed me over to the Council, they would still be eradicated. The Fae would still be taxed. The idea that he thought this war was something we could just give up on was laughable.

I turned away from the voice, and asked the trees to lift me up in the air so I could see the Council. They resisted at first, knowing from my mind what I was about to do, but finally a branch wrapped around my waist, and lifted me high in the air.

I could see the entire battle from there. The Council guards were surrounded by the supernatural army and the Fae rebels. I couldn't see anyone's faces, so I had no idea how my family was doing. Were they still alive?

Grey's reassurance flooded through the bond. He was still there. He was fighting in the war with his people. He would protect my family from the Council the best he could.

I sent back all the love and regret in my heart. Confusion came back to me and then his terror. I did my best to shut down the link. There was a definite possibility just as Ash had said that I might not make it out of the spell alive, but I had to do it.

It also hadn't been the best idea to distract my mate while he was in the middle of battle. I scanned the battlefield again but couldn't pinpoint him. He was still out there somewhere fighting for us, and pride flooded me.

My mate bond was strong, and if by some twist of Fate the spell didn't kill me, I would tell him just how much I loved him and how proud I was that he was mine.

The book flared with magic as I began the chant. It was difficult, but I had been practicing the words inside my head all afternoon. Magic poured from me as I stared at the Council members surrounded by their guards. They had a protective shield around them, but it wouldn't stop the binding spell from hitting them.

I started at a whisper but subtly grew louder as the spell called for it. I never took my eyes off the Council. The weakest members began to fidget and were shuffling their feet nervously. They knew something was happening. I would have smirked, but I was yelling, the chant now pouring every ounce of magic into the spell.

Ronaldo's eyes widened in terror, and the expression on his face was priceless. He knew what I was doing. I was too far away to hear his whispered words as I continued my chanting, but I thought he mouthed the words *the book* before he turned in my direction.

He glared at me as I continued chanting the words to the spell. Why was it taking so long?

Several of the Council elders dropped to their knees, but not Ronaldo or the main assholes from my trial. They remained standing huddled together and whispering to each other.

Did they think they had a way to stop this? The chant was almost completed. They would be bound until trial very soon.

"Get her!" Ronaldo's voice echoed through the battlefield as he pointed to me up in the tree, out of the way.

Our armies had already formed a wall around the Council's army, and I was outside it. I glanced down at Ash, but he was fighting off a glassy-eyed guard who must have slipped through our defenses.

The tide of the battle shifted, and the guards charged toward me. I continued the incantation, not afraid in the least. The trees wouldn't let anyone get to me.

By the time they did get close, the chant would be done. I poured all my magic into the words until something inside me cracked, and pain arced through my chest. I stared Ronaldo and the others down as they wailed and dropped to their knees.

I leaned into the trunk of the tree and slumped to my ass on the branch. I placed a hand on the trunk but didn't hear anything. I couldn't talk to the trees anymore. That was disappointing, but I'd finished the spell to stop the Council. I blinked, but I couldn't keep my eyes open. They were too heavy.

The pain in my chest was gone as well. I floated away into the clouds and closed my eyes again. I was content in the knowledge that I'd done it. I'd stopped the Council once and for all. My father would be able to try them for their crimes and usher in the new era.

My heart slowed its steady rhythm, and I was at peace with the knowledge that I'd succeeded, and the world would be safe once again.

Even if I died up there alone in the tree, the world would be safe, and my family would help make it so.

I closed my eyes and let unconsciousness take me even as a smile tugged at the corners of my lips. We'd done it. It was over.

Chapter 24

GREY

A COUNCIL WARRIOR lunged for me but stopped before his sword hit mine and crumpled to his knees, holding his head.

All around me warriors were doing the same. Ronaldo screamed, and I wasn't sure if it was from pain or fury. Why did they all suddenly fall? The few Council guards that were left ran, closing ranks around the Council, but it was no use. One by one, the men on the ground got up and turned on the Council.

Did Aurelia do that? Was that the spell? If it was, it was a waste, because we still had to fight the Council themselves. She could release the warriors from mind control without the spell though, so that couldn't be all she did.

I stalked toward the Council as their warriors realized something was wrong and sifted out, fleeing to let the Council deal with this alone.

"My magic. She stole my magic!" Ronaldo roared.

He held out his hands to blast me, but nothing happened. Aurelia had done that. She'd somehow left the Council powerless. I grinned as Fenrick strolled up next to me.

"My mate is a badass." I clapped him on the shoulder.

"That she is. Where is the princess?" He glanced around.

"Ash is with her. We need to arrest these assholes."

Dan rushed over and tossed me a backpack. "That should hold them until we can get them in the cells."

I opened the bag to find several sets of magic binding cuffs inside. It was probably overkill, considering they had no magic, but I didn't want to take any chances. The mind-controlled warriors all had their swords out, surrounding the Council as they waited for orders.

"I've got this." I stepped in front of Ronaldo, the absolute worst of all the Council members, and shoved him to his knees. "I should kill you here and now for all the atrocities you've committed."

"Do it, then," Ronaldo goaded me, his head still high even while he was on his knees.

"The very least I should do is kill you for the imprisonment and torture of my father for centuries, but my mate is right. The people deserve justice more than anything. That's why you're under arrest."

I clapped cuffs on his wrists behind his back, and Fenrick grabbed another set of cuffs and clapped them on another man.

"Those are useless." Ronaldo laughed. "Your mate probably died binding our magic with that book."

I hit Ronaldo in the back of the head, and he fell to the ground with his face in the dirt. I reached for the bond, but it was quiet. It hadn't been silent since we'd formed that bond. I scanned the battlefield for any sign of her, but she was nowhere to be found.

She couldn't be dead. She wouldn't have performed that spell knowing it might kill her, right?

"Where is she?" I asked Fenrick. "Do you see her?"

There were wounded everywhere from both sides, but I couldn't think about them. I needed to find my mate.

"Get cuffs on the Council members and get them to the cells," I ordered Dan as I stomped away.

I passed a group of shifters standing over a Fae warrior. He had a slash through his side, and they were trying to help him stop the bleeding. Now that the war was over, my people were helping the wounded without discrimination. That was what I liked to see.

I stomped past them toward a larger group of supernaturals. "Have any of you seen Aurelia?"

They shook their heads but parted, and I rushed over to them. The king lay wounded on the ground. I dropped to my knees next to him. His breath was rattling.

"Poison," he whispered. "The blade was poisoned."

"Shit. Where's the queen?" I turned to the group of shifters.

"She stayed back to keep the young ones calm," one of the witches said.

"Someone get her, now!" I barked.

Emotions clogged my throat. The king couldn't die. Aurelia would be devastated. She would be, because she was alive. There was no other explanation. She had to be alive.

I gripped the king's hand as one of the men shifted and ran back to the building to do as I'd commanded.

"Where's Aurelia?" The king coughed.

Blood stained his lips, and I wiped them clean. He was really dying. What the hell would we do without the king?

"I don't know. I was looking for her when I came across you." I rubbed my forehead. "Ash is with her. He'll keep her safe."

I had to believe that. No other outcome was acceptable to me. She had to be alive.

"You two will have to rule," the king whispered.

He was fading fast. Fenrick rushed to me and dropped to his knees. "What happened?"

"Poison," I said. "The Council must have ordered the king's death and sent an assassin into the battle to take him out with poison."

"Fuck," Fenrick growled. "Where's the queen?"

"Sent a shifter to get her from the bunker, but I'm not sure she's going to make it in time." I covered my face with my hands.

Showing any kind of emotion was difficult but losing the king like this hurt. It was going to devastate my mate. The queen ran toward us, screaming with tears streaming down her face. I turned away and coughed to disguise the lump building in my throat.

The king had become a friend. Was this how Aurelia had felt when my father died in front of her? The crushing despair wracked me. Tears burned the backs of my eyes. The queen wailed as she fell to the ground at the king's side.

His eyes cracked open, and he smiled. I couldn't take any more of this. It felt too personal to watch their final goodbye. I stood up and scanned the battlefield again. Many of the mind-controlled Fae were leaning over supernaturals, using their healing abilities to help the wounded.

I still couldn't find Aurelia. "Where the hell is she?"

I rushed back to the wards. She was back behind the battle lines. I'd made sure she wouldn't get close enough to the Council, but did she listen? A crowd had formed at the wards, and I prayed to whatever gods that were listening that they weren't crowded around my mate's body.

I grabbed a supernatural that was running past me. He stopped in his tracks and bowed his head to me.

"Have you seen the princess?" I asked.

"No, my king. I haven't seen her since before the battle." He glanced down at my hand, and I released him.

I spun back toward the crowd and stomped to them, but the mass parted, and a somber Ash was in front of me. My body buzzed with electricity and my wolf whimpered and howled in my head. I glanced down at the bundle he carried gently in his arms.

The world spun around me, and I bellowed with rage as I dropped to the ground. What had she done? No, this couldn't be the outcome. It couldn't. Magic pulsed beneath my skin. We were bonded. If she died, I was supposed to be taken with her.

What kind of cruel trick had Fate dealt me that she was so still in Ash's arms? "No, no. This isn't acceptable."

"I'm sorry, Grey," Ash whispered.

I'd never seen so much emotion on the Rider's face. Not even when we'd had to leave his brother with the Council. Wetness pooled around his eyes and a single tear fell down his cheek. He crouched down in front of me with Aurelia still cradled in his arms.

The magic in my veins roared inside me, desperate to get out. What would happen if I let it out? I would burn the world. I'd told her that if I lost her, the world would have a new monster to deal with.

I tugged her out of Ash's lap and fell back on my ass in the grass. I inhaled deeply through my nose, filling my senses with her beautiful scent. I buried my face in her hair and sobbed.

My chest burned with regret, anger, despair and probably a few emotions I couldn't name. I squeezed her close and rocked us on the grass as my magic continued to push at the boundaries of my chest.

It wanted out, but there was nothing it could do in this situation. Aurelia's eyes were closed, and I kissed each lid softly. She couldn't be gone.

The magic building inside of me leaked out through my palms where I was touching her and glowed gold against her skin. I glanced at the magic, not wanting it to harm her even though she was already gone. I panicked and tried to pull it back, but it rushed out with my emotion and flooded Aurelia with warmth.

"I told her I would ride across the veil and bring her back if she died." Ash choked out the words.

His head was down, and he swiped at his eyes. Was the Rider crying like I was? He didn't see the magic pouring out of me into her. The magic was angry, but I realized it wasn't dangerous. Her skin changed back to her usual healthy glow before my eyes, and my mate gasped for breath as her eyes shot open.

"Grey?" she croaked.

She lifted a hand to my face. My mouth hung open, and words escaped me as I stared at her beautiful eyes. The bond flared back to life, and her relief and love filled me.

"You're alive," I sobbed and pulled her closer, never wanting her to leave my sight again.

That was too much to bear. How the hell did I save her? Magic couldn't bring people back from the dead. My magic hadn't even reacted to the king's death. Why did it react so violently to hers?

"What happened?" she asked as she laid her head on my shoulder. "Did we win?"

"Yes, Princess," Ash chuckled and swiped at his tears. "But if you ever do that again, I'll lock you in a padded room for the rest of your days."

"Agreed. I'll help," I said as I nuzzled her neck where my mate mark was displayed.

"It worked? The Council's magic is bound, and you brought me back?" Aurelia cupped my cheek. "How?"

"I don't know. I was lost in my grief, and my magic flared. It poured into you, and then you woke up." I shook my head.

It sounded crazy when I said it out loud, but there was no real explanation for it. She was there, and we'd won the war. The Council would be tried for their crimes, and we could figure out a way to work with the humans.

"Where are the others? My father—is he okay?"

Fenrick jogged over with a frown and dropped to his knees. He bowed his head, but his eyes were red and glassy. "The king is gone, Your Majesty."

Aurelia gasped and tried to jump from my arms, but I held her to me. I wasn't ready to let go of her yet.

"He can't be gone!" she cried. "Don't call me majesty, Fenrick."

"I'm sorry, Aurelia, but before he left this world for the beyond, he stated that you would rule. Now. Together." Fenrick nodded my direction.

A Shifter King mated to a Fae queen... maybe that was how we were to usher in a new era. Our people would all be safe in Faery, and free from oppression.

We'd lost a good king that day, but the future was looking brighter than ever as long as we could work with the humans.

Chapter 25

AURELIA

"WHY ARE WE DOING THIS NOW?" I asked over my shoulder.

"My queen, we have been over this. The people need some light after all the dark." Magna grinned.

Grey stepped next to me in a suit that looked sinful on him and kissed my cheek.

"Right after the coronation, we have a meeting with the world leaders in the human realm. You want to be seen as the magnanimous queen you are. And not everyone knows I'll be your king. We need to show a united front."

"Not everyone agrees with your decision to let the other supernaturals and the half breeds return. They need to see that they're wrong, and bigotry will not be tolerated." Magna nodded.

"I understand." I stood in front of the mirror in a gold gown that would have been all the rage in the regency period.

The crown was in the throne room on a dais, waiting for the ceremony. We'd brought some technology to Faery and were going to live stream to all the towns so they could see the event. It had taken us weeks to get everything set up.

I hated it because every day that passed was another day that Zeke and the others stayed in the detention facilities. I needed to bring our people home. Grey walked up behind me and placed his hands on my bare shoulders.

"It will be okay, my love. We just need to get through the ceremony and then have a chat with the humans." Grey squeezed my shoulders and pressed a chaste kiss to my cheek.

"It's time," Magna said with a grin.

"Finally. Let's get this over with," I groaned.

"The king needs to go out first. Asher and Fenrick will escort you," Magna said, shooing Grey out of the room.

I hated that my parents weren't going to be with me for this ceremony but that was the nature of a coronation. Kings rarely gave up their thrones in Faery. They were almost always claimed by someone's death. My mother would be with my father, sitting at his side as she always did.

Grey winked at me over his shoulder as he left our room. Magna closed the door firmly behind him.

"This is what you were leading us to, wasn't it?" I asked the seer.

"Not quite, but we're almost there." There was a twinkle of mischief in her eyes.

"There's more?" I asked with a sigh.

"Not for you, Princess. Your story has its happy ending, but others are just beginning."

"You and your riddles." I shook my head.

The doors opened, and Fenrick stood in front of me. He bowed deeply, and I scowled at him.

"Stop that," I scolded.

Fenrick stood with a laugh. "Are you ready to be escorted to your coronation?"

"I would rather be getting our people out of the testing centers but sure, let's go." I waved a hand.

Magna rolled her eyes but followed behind me to make sure the long train on my dress fanned out just right.

"The ceremony won't take long." Fenrick held his arm out to me.

I looped my arm through his, and smiled at Ash as I did the same with him. "Let's get this over with so we can save our people."

"Agreed," Ash said.

He was the only one who'd agreed with me that we needed to secure our people before the coronation. He wanted Zeke back as much as I did if not more, but we were overruled by the needs of many.

I could see their point, but I also didn't like the idea of my people suffering unnecessarily. If I could help them quickly, I wanted to do it.

"You know the human government wouldn't take you seriously unless you were the actual queen." Fenrick squeezed my hand.

I huffed out a breath. This was the same argument we'd had for weeks, and I got it. But it didn't make me happy.

Supernaturals and Fae lined the hall leading to the throne room and when they saw me, everyone dropped to one knee. That wasn't weird at all. Especially when we got to the rest of Ash and Zeke's brothers, and they were kneeling as well.

"Get up," I whispered to the Riders. "What are you doing?"

"They are showing respect to their queen," Ash whispered in my ear.

I nodded and allowed Ash and Fenrick to lead me into the throne room where Grey stood at the door. We'd been practicing this for weeks. I just had to promise to uphold the laws and protect my people, and then I would be crowned.

It was simple and would only take a matter of minutes, but it was tradition and mattered to the people of the realm. I took a cleansing breath and smiled at Grey as he reached for my hand. We both made our way down the aisle lined with friends and family until we got to the steps of the throne.

We knelt there and said a prayer to the gods that they would bless our reign before standing. Grey helped me sit in the seat of my father. It was something we'd discussed at length. He'd said I should be the head of government since my father was king and I'd saved the supernaturals in the war.

I hadn't actually agreed, but outwardly to everyone we would have these roles though we would make decisions together.

The high priest asked us to give our vows to our people and then we said another prayer to the gods for their blessing before the crowns were placed on each of our heads. The crowd exploded in cheers and applause as we hurried from the throne room into the surveillance room we had off to the side.

"Are the world leaders on the call yet?" I asked the tech.

"They aren't, but you are a couple minutes early." He grinned.

He gripped a microphone and handed it to Grey. Grey clipped it carefully to my dress and the shifter handed me a set of ear pods. He clicked a few buttons, and we were ready for the video call.

A few moments later, the President came on the screen. "You."

He pointed a finger accusingly but did a double take when he saw the crown on my head.

"Mr. President. You have something that belongs to me, and I want it back." I glared at him.

"I have something of yours? I don't have anything that belongs to you. You were supposed to be tried for the explosion of the prison. How are you suddenly wearing a crown?"

"I would mind my tone and show respect for the new queen of Faery if I were you," Grey snapped.

The President glanced at Grey next to me and his eyes widened. I guess he didn't know who the new ruling monarchs of Faery would be.

"Look, before this meeting devolves any further, you have my people locked in your testing facilities and I want them back," I said placing a hand on Grey's arm.

"No," the President said.

"No?" I asked, cocking my head to the side.

"I have citizens of the United States locked in detention facilities. They are mine to punish as I see fit."

"Your citizens? Punished? What crimes have they committed? You detained them because they weren't human, and as such had no human rights, but now you claim they are your citizens, and you can punish them for existing as you see fit?" I asked and glanced at Grey. "Am I hearing this right?"

"You are, my love. It's the most hypocritical bullshit I've ever heard spewed in my life." Grey sat forward, glaring at the President.

"We need to come to an agreement. All supernaturals are welcome back into Faery, but I will not force them to come back. Some still have families in the human realm. I need to know that they will be safe to return there without persecution."

"Monsters will always be labeled monsters. They will never be welcome to live among humans." The President slammed his fist on the desk in front of him.

I glanced at Grey warily. He nodded, knowing what I was asking without words.

"If you don't release my people from your detention centers, I will have no choice but to attack those centers and free them. I will send as many teams as necessary, and they will make the explosion at the Dallas prison look like a bonfire." I raised a brow.

"Where is the High Councilor?" the President barked. "I only deal with him."

"He is currently on trial for his crimes against my people. I expect to sentence him to death very soon." I smirked.

"Who gave you the authority to sentence him to death?" The President's face turned an ugly eggplant color.

"My people and the gods themselves just witnessed my coronation." I grinned. "As the Princess of the Shadow Kingdom, I was next in line when the Council assassinated my father."

The President went pale. "I didn't know the Fae had royalty."

"You were given wrong information. The Council used you and controlled your peoples' minds to do their bidding. They will be punished, but that's not why I'm talking with you now. I want my people released from the detention facilities, and I want you to pass legislation to make any supernatural who stays in the realm a citizen and keep them safe."

"That's not possible. The American people are terrified of the threat the supernaturals pose to us. We cannot let them roam free." He slammed his fist on the table again as another world leader popped onto the screen.

I glanced at Grey for guidance. I didn't know who the woman was.

"Hello, Mrs. Prime Minister," Grey greeted her warmly. "Have you had a chance to look at the proposal we sent over?"

The Prime Minister smiled at Grey and nodded. "It was all very reasonable. If the supernaturals in the UK act up, they will be sent back to Faery to be tried for their crimes. We will release everyone in our custody to you, but they will have the option to stay or go."

"Has your parliament decided on a plan of action?" I asked.

The President scoffed but I ignored him. The British Prime Minister seemed more reasonable and pleasant to talk to.

"We have decided that we would rather work with you than start a possible war with the supernatural. We will agree to your terms." She nodded, and I sighed with relief.

If only the other world leaders would be that easy to work with. I glared at the screen with the President. He'd heard the conversation with the British Prime Minister, and his purple complexion grew darker.

"You, Mr. President, have my family locked in your testing centers and I refuse to leave them there to die. I don't want a war with the US. It was my home for the majority of my life, but I will take out every one of your facilities if it comes down to it. Take your pick."

The British Prime Minister gasped. "Carl, let her people go. They aren't a threat to you."

"No, I will keep her people and any other supernaturals found on US soil. They aren't human, and we need to know more about them, Bridget. I'm surprised you gave into their demands so easily."

"We don't want war with these people, Carl," the Prime Minister hissed.

Maybe that was exactly what the President wanted, but we would avoid it at all costs. Somehow, we would get our people out of those centers. We had to. There was no other acceptable option.

"We don't want to start a war either. Give us our people back and we can come to an agreement," I said with a raised brow.

We'd saved the supernaturals and the realms, but we still had a long way to go for peace. I hoped Asher didn't go rogue and attempt to release Zeke. That could start a war we weren't ready for.

Epilogue
GREY

5 YEARS LATER...

A SCREAM TORE through the castle. I clung tightly to my son Christian as I raced through the empty hall. "You think it's time?"

"Time." Christian nodded seriously.

The future king of the realm was a serious little tyke, much like his grandfather was. He frowned and his bottom lip quivered as another wail pierced my eardrums.

"Aurelia," I called out, my stomach twisting with worry.

"Grey?" Her whimper came from our bedroom as I turned the corner.

My beautiful mate was doubled over holding her rounded belly in the doorway. "My love, get back into bed."

I set Christian down on the floor and he toddled over to his mother putting his hand on her stomach. "Sissy."

"Yes Christian, but we need Mommy to lay down for sissy to come out." I ruffled his blond hair and used calm tones.

Bright blue eyes blinked up at me and he glanced back at his mom. "Rest."

Aurelia stared at our boy and forced a small smile to her lips. Her breathing was labored and she winced as pain tore through her again.

I wrapped my arm around her back and bent forward, picking her up in a bridal hold to carry her back into the bedroom. Christian followed close behind me and jumped on the bed when I laid Aurelia down.

He snuggled next to her with his tiny hand on her huge belly.

"I need to call the healer." I glanced down at Christian. "Protect mommy and sissy until I get back."

He nodded seriously again, his understanding of what I needed from him showing once more that he was much older than his years suggested.

I turned around and raced from the room, running into Fenrick who stood in the hall on high alert.

"What's happened to the queen?" he asked, his eyebrows snapping together.

"It's time for the babies to come." I ran a hand down my face, trying to keep it together.

"The first set of twins in the history of Faery is going to be a celebration. Why do you look so uneasy?" he asked.

"I'm always uneasy when she's in pain," I said with a shake of my head.

When Christian was born three years ago, I was a complete wreck. Today was no different.

"Everything will be fine, Grey. She's strong." Fenrick clapped me on the shoulder.

"I get that. But that doesn't stop the wolf inside me from pacing around inside me causing my stress to double. I need to find the healer." I raced down the hall.

The healer should have been ready and waiting by Aurelia's side. We'd known the birth would be any day now. We'd found out just how short a hybrid pregnancy could be with Christian's arrival. She was pregnant for only five months instead of the expected nine and with twins we knew that would be even more accelerated.

I pounded on the door to the healer's room. How did they not hear my mate screaming when everyone else did?

"Can I help you, my king?"

I jumped and turned around, seeing the healer rounding the corner as she walked calmly towards me.

"Where have you been?" I roared. "The queen is in labor and you are supposed to be there."

"I'm sorry, my king. I needed to go to the village for supplies." She bowed her head and hurried off to find the queen.

I groaned and marched after her, Fenrick grabbing my arm as I tried to push past him.

"You need to calm down, Grey." Fenrick said, slapping me on the back.

"I can't calm down when I can feel her pain." I clenched my fists at my sides.

"If you act like a raging bull to the healer in there, I will remove you. Your mate needs a calm presence at her side, not whatever the fuck this is." He huffed, crossing his arms to show me he was serious.

Another wave of pain stole my breath. My mate bellowed her agony from the bed and I raced into the bedroom.

"Grey," Aurelia gasped out, then whimpered again. "It hurts."

"I know, my love, but you're doing so well." I sat on the bed next to her and brushed the hair away from her forehead.

The healer cleared her throat. "It will all be over soon, my queen. I just need to lock on their energy so I can get them out."

We'd watched some videos of human births when Aurelia was pregnant with Christian, thinking that would prepare us better. We couldn't have been more wrong. Human labor was is nothing like Fae births.

The healer rested her palm on Aurelia's stomach and hummed to herself as she furrowed her brow. "Got her."

With a burst of green magic and light, the first of the twins was in my arms. She was a wriggling, wet mess, but she was also incredibly beautiful. I stared down at her, holding her tight against my chest. Her hair was a soft chestnut color and her big blue eyes stared up at me.

"Sissy," Christian called out, crawling over to me across the bed.

He placed a kiss on the baby's cheek. He was going to be such an amazing big brother to our girls. I couldn't wait to see them all grow.

I turned to Aurelia and presented our newest addition to our growing family. Her eyes glowed with love for the tiny infant.

"Dahlia," she whispered, reaching out to brush her fingers against the girl's cheek.

"One more to go," the healer said.

She placed her hand on Aurelia's stomach again and my mate winced. I glared at the healer but she didn't pay any attention to me. More green magic pulsed through the air and the other twin was suddenly nestled in her mother's arms.

"Kenzie," Aurelia said pressing a kiss to the girl's hair.

The twins were identical, and perfect. I heaved a sigh of relief moments before the worries came flooding in. What kind of mischief would the two of them get up to?

"We are going to have problems with these two beauties." I said, shaking my head.

"Maybe when they get older it will be easier to tell them apart," Aurelia said, staring down at the baby in her arms.

"Hopefully," I grumbled, already afraid of what was to come.

I stood up from the bed and rocked the infant in my arms. The healer was still using her magic on Aurelia to heal any internal damage that the babies may have caused. Dahlia stared up at me, my precious princess. She scrunched her nose up as if she can hear my thoughts.

"We make some beautiful babies, mate." I turned my grin on the love of my life, a woman who's helped me save our world and our people.

Aurelia was my match in every way. I couldn't wait to spend the rest of eternity with her.

AURELIA

FIVE YEARS EVEN LATER...

"Those girls are as impossible to catch as you were," Fenrick grumbled.

"You asked to be the twins' guardian, Fenrick." I grinned back at him. "What did you expect?"

He ran a hand down his face. "I expected that they would stay the sweet little princesses they were as babies. Not this reign of terror."

Christian stomped into the throne room his eyes blazing with anger. "Where's Dahlia?"

"She and Kenzie are off somewhere causing chaos again, why?" I asked.

"She broke my tablet. I know it was her because I have to tell her ten times a day that it's mine and she can't play with it."

"I did not." Dahlia jumped out from behind my throne crossing her pudgy arms and glaring back at Christian.

"It didn't just end up broken for no reason," Christian argued.

"Enough," I snapped, struggling not to roll my eyes. "You have your own tablet Dahlia. You know you're not supposed to touch other people's stuff without asking."

My children were as willful as they were stubborn, but with Grey and I as their parents, I didn't expect anything less..

"I didn't break it, though." Dahlia repeated, and I actually believed her this time. But they needed to be allies, not enemies.

"We'll get you a new tablet and your sister won't touch it, will you?" I glanced at the chestnut haired little spitfire.

Dahlia was only five and already she and her sister were a handful. They really needed a guardian each, but Fenrick was one of the best and even he had trouble keeping up with them.

The doors to the throne room burst open and Ash steps through the door with his arms out wide. "Where are my favorite princesses?"

"Uncle Ash!" Dahlia yelled and Kenzie popped up on the other side of my throne and rushed towards Asher.

They so rarely got to see Ash nowadays since he lived in the mortal world. So when he did come to visit the kids, they were all filled with excitement. I stood up and watched as my girl's chattered on to their Uncle Ash, who had a big grin on my face.

Even though Ash and the other riders of the hunt weren't technically family they were like brothers to me. Arms wrapped around my body from behind and pulled me into a broad chest.

"You're all smiles." Grey kissed my neck over his mark.

"They were fighting again, then Ash came in and it's completely forgotten." I leaned my head back on his shoulder with a sigh.

"I doubt it's completely forgotten." Grey chuckled, pointing at Christian's stormy face.

He was shooting subtle glares at the twins when Ash wasn't looking. I shook my head. This would probably get mentioned every time he got mad at his sister for the rest of eternity.

"You're right but at least for this moment we have a little peace." I turned in his arms and stared up into his gorgeous face. Even after all these years, I ached for his touches.

"I wouldn't change a thing." Grey pulled me closer to his hard chest. "Our girls are chaos gremlins and will be a force of nature when they grow up, but they are perfect. Christian is a little broody but he's mine so that's to be expected."

"You were definitely broody when we first met." I agreed, kissing his lips gently.

A chorus of ew's filled the throne room and I giggled as Grey deepened the kiss. When he finally pulled away again, he didn't leave me. Instead, he pressed his forehead to mine.

"I was broody, but a strong-willed fae princess changed me for the better. One day Christian will find someone too and he will be changed forever too."

"Let's not get ahead of ourselves," I rushed to say. I didn't even want to think about the day that my babies moved on. "They're still children and I want to keep them small as long as I can."

"Of course, my love."

Our life was chaotic and messy sometimes but it also amazing. Growing up, sleeping on the carpet inside a wardrobe... those days seemed so far away now.

I would never take my babies, or my mate for granted, and if I was brutally honest, I wouldn't change my family for anything in the world. They were mine and I was there's and there wasn't a thing in this world that would take that away from me.

THE END

I hope you enjoyed the last of the Wicked Fae series. I am thinking about writing a spin off series about The Riders of the Hunt- but those ideas are still ruminating within my mind.

Until then... have you read my Shifter Rejected series?
Book 1 is FREE and you can download it here:
https://books2read.com/wolfofash
Otherwise here is a sneak peak into book 1- Wolf of Ash.

Chapter 1

TALIA

IN SIX DAYS, I was marrying the next Alpha of the Northwood pack. Maddox Brady. My fated mate.

Lights flashed around me and the room spun with the beat of the heavy techno music the DJ was playing. I didn't dare get up from the stool where I teetered, lest I fall flat on my face. Yet, despite my intoxication, the simple fact was, I'd never been happier. I loved Maddox and couldn't wait to marry him.

"Another round of tequila shots!" I called to the bartender, though I wasn't sure he'd bring them. He'd said something about cutting us off earlier, but surely he'd been joking?

"You can't handle another round, Talia," said Nyssa, my best friend.

I leaned forward on my stool and straightened my pink and white sash. We all had them. Mine read, 'Bride-to-be'.

"This is my last night as a single lady!" I sang the words, amazed at how loud I could be when the music thumped around me like a drum in my ear. "Gotta make every minute count."

Nyssa laughed. "The mating ceremony's not for another week, Talia. You've still got time."

"Here, I got you another one," Celia whispered, handing me a small glass of clear liquor. My other best friend had come through for me.

I took the drink, my hand wobbling as I brought it to my lips. I snorted, then tipped my head back, throwing the shot down my throat.

"Wow." I grimaced at the burn, and handed Celia back the glass. Then I took a deep breath and focused on the warm feeling of the alcohol spreading through my veins.

Oh, yeah. That has to be the last one. Or I'll never make it home.

Thank goodness the wedding was next week and not tomorrow.

Then again, if it *was* tomorrow, I would never have gotten this smashed.

"Are you excited for the wedding night?" Nyssa asked me, wiggling her eyebrows up and down.

Celia snickered, while I rolled my eyes. They all knew I couldn't wait to finally consummate my relationship with Maddox.

My fated mate.

My true love.

The future Alpha of our pack.

"Of course, she is!" Celia answered for me.

Celia was my oldest friend. We'd known each other practically from the day we'd been born. Her mom and mine were friends from way back, and we'd been raised together as more sisters, than anything else.

Celia turned to me with an eyebrow raised. She was by far the most sober of us. "You never told us what the real reason was."

I leaned forward on the bar stool, careful not to crush the peanuts lying on the surface of the bar top, then squinted at my friend. "For what?"

Celia glared at me. "For waiting this long to have sex with him!"

I gasped at her forwardness, then put a hand over my mouth and giggled.

I shook my head, not wanting to answer.

She jabbed me in the arm with her finger and I swayed on my seat. "Whoa..."

"Come on, Talia! You can tell us!"

Nyssa nodded. "Yeah. I want to know why, too."

I hefted my top for the tenth time, trying to cover up the ridiculous amount of cleavage this outfit showed off to the room, and shrugged.

"We just... decided to wait."

I didn't want to admit it hadn't been my decision. Maddox had been adamant though. We needed to get married first.

Celia pulled another stool over to the bar and huddled closer so she could hear me better. The music was loud, and the people dancing and drinking on this warm summer night were even louder.

I closed my eyes, enjoying the heat of the room and the warmth in my blood. As the next Alpha's mate, I was watched constantly when we were at home. In the pack. In town. At formal gatherings.

I tried to be as perfect as possible. For Maddox. For the current Alpha of the Northwood pack. And also for my dad.

But tonight was my bachelorette party. I could finally let down my hair and not worry about anyone else and what they might think of me.

The steady beat and thump of one of my favorite songs came through the speakers. I jumped to my unsteady feet, wobbling on the tiny heels Nyssa had made me wear.

"Let's dance!"

I pulled my two best friends to the dance floor. They were my entire bridal party and all I needed. I began to sway and twerk and giggle away.

This wasn't my last night of freedom, of course. But it was one of my last nights as a single woman. Soon I would be a mate, a wife, and the future Alpha's mate, with all the responsibilities that came with that position.

And I couldn't wait.

"Is Maddox doing his bachelor party tonight too?" Celia asked, dancing forward to whisper the question into my ear.

I twirled toward her. "Doesn't matter, 'cos I'm here with you!"

I grabbed her hands and spun around, almost falling on my ass, but managing to stay on my feet.

Just.

We laughed and danced, and drank more, thanks to Celia.

Close to dawn, we all caught a cab back to the pack, then staggered into the house I shared with my father.

"Your dad doesn't mind if we stay over?" Celia asked, throwing her dress to the floor and crawling into my bed with her underwear still in place.

I dragged the curtains shut, blocking out the rising sun. "'Course not. You guys are family."

The girls smiled as they settled on either side of the bed.

I took a drunken moment to appreciate how lucky I was to have these two in my life. As an only child, these girls were the closest thing I had to sisters.

I stripped off my own clothes, relieved when my short skirt and too-obvious top were in a pile on the floor. I enjoyed being pretty like every other girl, but boobs and legs on show everywhere was not usually my style.

"The house is really quiet. So is the rest of the town," Celia whispered, her eyes closing as she nestled into the pillow she'd landed on.

I crawled onto the king-sized bed and slid under the covers between my friends.

"Dad's out. He said there was some pack business thing they had to do today."

Nyssa huffed out a laugh as she rolled over. "You're the future Alpha's mate and you still don't get told anything, huh?"

"Yeah..." I lied, and closed my eyes.

I knew where they'd all gone, which was probably half the reason I'd drunk so much tonight. But we'd gotten on the water around two a.m., and now that I was well on the way to sober thanks to my wolf metabolism, the anxiety had set back in.

Maddox, my dad, and the rest of the men in our pack had planned an attack today. On a neighboring pack they considered a major threat.

The Long Claw Pack. Their Alpha was legendary for his strength, as was his son, Galen. Though I hadn't met either of them.

Personally, I hated the wars the wolves fought amongst

themselves. It didn't make sense to me when we had so many other natural enemies. We all had our own territories, so why wolves constantly fought for more power, was beyond me.

And I hated the fact that the men I loved put themselves in danger like this.

I rolled onto my side and let exhaustion sweep me away. I tried not to dream about the dangers my family were in. After all, my dad and Maddox were my whole world.

GALEN

My eyes sprung open at the sound of running footsteps thumping through my dad's house.

The door to my bedroom flung open and I sat bolt upright in bed.

"We're being raided." Oe of my betas, Tommy, pushed the door wide. "It's those fuckers from the Northwood Pack. They're here."

I jumped out of bed and rapidly pulled on some old jeans. One of the fifty pairs I kept for moments like this: when I knew I was going to shift, and probably destroy the clothing in a split second.

"Go," I told Tommy. "I'll be there straight away."

Tommy ran out the door again.

I didn't bother with a sweatshirt. This was going to be a fight, not a conversation. I didn't need to dress properly.

I chased after Tommy, ducking into my dad's room on the way, where he lay in his bed, fast asleep and as pale as the sheets he lay on. He had a light sheen of sweat decorating his brow.

Dad hadn't been well for months, so there was no way I was waking him now. If he knew they'd come, he'd want to join the fight, and in his current state, it was highly unlikely he'd survive. He could barely stand, let alone shift and defend our territory against a bunch of strong wolves.

I wasn't ready to be Alpha of my dad's Long Claw Pack. Not yet.

And I wasn't ready to live in a world without my dad in it.

"Galen!" Tommy hissed from the front door. "Come on!"

CHAPTER 1

I hightailed it out of my dad's room and reached the front door. "What do we know?"

"The Northwood Pack is about to attack. Our scouts have seen them coming through the woods."

"How many are there?" I asked, already mentally preparing for the fight we were about to have.

The neighboring pack had always hated our borders, though I wasn't sure why. There was bad blood from way back before I was born and no one had ever mentioned what happened back then.

But why attack? And why now?

Had they heard my father was dying and our pack would need to fight without our Alpha? That was the most likely explanation for this timing.

Assholes.

They thought we were weak without my dad. We'd just have to prove them wrong.

"At least thirty strong," Tommy said. "Maybe more."

I nodded once. They'd brought most of their pack. The men anyway.

I hope their Alpha is with them. I'd love to take him out. Or his pussy of a son. Maddox.

"Let's go."

I was next in line to my father, born from a long line of Alphas. I could lead our men in this fight. And, victorious, or not, I would never abandon them.

Tommy and I ran through the town, waking up our fellow pack mates and shouting out orders. "Lock the doors. Make sure your families remain safe."

All our women were strong fighters if need be, but it was their job to protect our children if something happened to the men.

It was our role to protect them, so that hopefully they'd never have to fight to save their babies.

I called to my Betas. "Let's get to the forest edge."

Our town was built well and was only vulnerable from two sides.

I had at least forty men, so I could afford to divide our forces.

"Split up! You five go to the east." It was unlikely the neighboring pack would attack that way. Their lands lay to the south. But I didn't want to leave any of our borders unmanned, just in case. "The rest of you follow me."

We ran to the south side, where the forest butted up against the town. My heart pounded like a war drum in my chest. Adrenaline zinged along my veins.

The only question in my mind was whether I needed to shift straight away, or later. We didn't carry weapons, but my claws were razor sharp, as were my teeth.

"There!" someone cried, and I squinted into the darkness of the forest.

The sun was only beginning to lift its head. Whisps of red and orange hues rose about the horizon, lighting up the blackened sky.

Deep in the forest, wolves stalked toward us. They'd already shifted, their beady yellow eyes standing out against the darkness around them.

Well, I'm not getting caught out with my fragile human body. They're clearly not here to talk. That's for damn certain.

I let go of my humanity. My wolf rose inside me, growling loudly as it took over.

I dropped to the ground onto all fours. My whole body vibrated as my skin sprouted fur, and I transformed into the huge beast of my forefathers.

My black wolf form.

And then it was on.

They charged, and every man around me shifted. The dawn filled with the snarls of the wolves from two packs—mine, and theirs.

There was no warm-up, no formalities, as the neighboring pack ran out of the woods toward us. This was going to be a fight to the death, and I damn sure wasn't going down today. Not on my land. Not on my father's death watch.

I flew at the nearest wolf rushing forward, my mouth open, teeth ready.

He snapped in my face, missing his mark as I twisted. I tore around the side of him, ripping my teeth through his fur and tasting blood on my tongue.

CHAPTER 1

The wolf yelped and skittered sideways, before teaming up with another gray wolf near him and coming back for a second try.

They both faced me, their lips raised in matching snarls. I charged, aiming for the new wolf, and head butted him, then bared my teeth to the one I'd already injured.

He should have run when he had the chance.

This time I grabbed him around the throat, my ears burning with his whimper a moment before I tore out his throat. Blood gushed into my mouth.

His neck snapped as he fell to the ground, his head tilted at an odd angle, and I turned to growl at the other wolf.

They'd come onto my land, into our town, to what? Kill us all? Even the women and children?

Not today.

The other wolf started to back away, before lifting his head and howling. It was a high-pitched sound that set my fur on edge. He was calling for help.

I charged, my mouth open, and sunk my teeth around the wolf's neck and shook him. Hard.

Enough to warn, not kill. If he came at me again, I wouldn't give him a second chance.

He scrabbled into the dirt to get away from me, and I let him.

He whined as he backed away, toward the forest.

I backed up a few steps also, watching as their pack rejoined forces and grouped together near the forest's edge once more.

Where was their leader?

There. A large black wolf who met my eyes. He was still in challenge mode, but he was wavering. I could read the uncertainty in his expression.

I stepped over body after body of dead wolves to get back to the rest of my pack. The guys, my betas, were blood-smeared and panting, but looked mostly okay.

I stood at the head of the Long Claw Pack and growled at the intruders that had come from the Northwood. It was their call. Would they regroup and try again, or would they turn tail and retreat? We wouldn't chase them if they chose the latter.

The large black wolf howled once, and as one, the whole pack turned away. Their Alpha, the one in charge, had called an end to the fight.

Good decision.

I let myself begin to relax. They were leaving.

Then suddenly, a large gray wolf growled and broke away from the retreating group, running around their pack to head straight at me.

This lone wolf was trying to take me out? Seriously?

But he wasn't alone for long. As he ran, others followed, until he'd managed to pull several wolves away from the main pack. They were all coming toward me now.

I shook my head as I faced them.

Idiots.

They'd just lessened the numbers of their main group by ten, all the while bringing the party to me. Perfect.

I dug my feet into the dirt and launched at them.

Then the whole pack came at us. They'd obviously decided to join the second wave.

We fought hard, and I killed two more of their wolves before the other side called another retreat.

I stared after them as the remaining wolves ran for their lives through the woods, back the way they had come. In that second attack, they'd lost at least five more pack members, and I almost growled at the stupidity of it all.

I let go of my shifter, rising from my animal posture to stand on two feet again.

My naked skin was covered in sweat and my heart thumped loudly in my chest as the adrenaline took time to dissipate.

"Should we go after them?" Markus asked, having transformed back to human beside me. He was huffing and puffing from exertion.

Blood poured down his chest from a wound in his shoulder.

I shook my head. "We will avenge this attack, but not today. Right now, we patch up our injured, and burn the bodies of their fallen."

They'd gotten what they deserved, coming onto our land to try and kill us while we slept. They had twelve dead, if I counted correctly, and many others of them had been injured. A huge hit to any pack. They were weaker now. There would be no coming back until they regrouped, which gave me time to plan our attack.

I glanced around at my own pack members. Several injured, and two dead.

There would be justice. Our pack would have its vengeance.

Continue reading 'Wolf of Ash' for FREE at all retailers and you can download it here:
https://books2read.com/wolfofash

Printed in Great Britain
by Amazon